CATSKILLS CAPERS BOOK 2

Mountain Maître D' Mystery

Lily Barrish Levner

Neversink Press

*In loving memory of my aunt Linda Barrish Zwerner
and my father-in-law Howie Levner*

Yiddish Dictionary

Ay, Ay, Ay: oh, woe! or oh, joy!
Alta cocker: older person
Alte makh sheyfe: old witch
Bashert: meant to be
Boychik: boy
Bubbe: grandmother
Bruchas: blessing/prayer
Bimmies: (not a Yiddish word) hotel workers on the lower end of the hotel ladder that did menial jobs
Bubalah: sweetheart or darling
Chutzpah: audacity, confidence and a little impudence
Dummkopf: foolish person
Es gezinteheit: eat in good health
Fakakta: lousy, crappy, ridiculous
Fleishigs: meat-based meal
Farshtunken: nasty, smelly
Gelt: money
Geshmak: delicious
Gonsa macher: big, important person
Goy: non-Jewish person
Gute meydl: good girl
Heimish: homey, cozy
Kaddish: Jewish prayer said in honor of the dead
Keppie: head
Kibitzing: chat
Kinder: children
Kreplach: soup dumplings
Kuchalein: boarding house, with one shared kitchen

Kvelling: bursting with pride
Kvetch: whining/complaining
Makhasheyfe: witch
Mandelbroit: almond bread
Mazel tov: congratulations or good luck
Mensch: person of integrity
Meshuga: crazy
Milkhik: dairy-based meal
Minyan: quorum of ten adult Jewish men required for religious obligations and prayers
Nebbish: regarded as pitiful or "poor thing"
Nosh: snack or eat lightly
Nu: versatile expression that can mean so? well? What's up? So what?
Oy vey: (oh, woe!) dismay, frustration, grief
Putz: foolish/jerk
Schlep: drag or carry
Schmaltz: rendered chicken fat
Schmata: rag
Schmear: to spread
Schmooze: chat
Schmuck: obnoxious person
Schmendrick: foolish or inept person
Schtick: act/gimmick/trick/prank
Shabbat: Jewish day of rest
Shabbat Shalom: Sabbath greeting
Shabbos: Jewish Sabbath
Shanda: same or disgrace
Shayna: beautiful
Shtetl: little town
Shtick drek: piece of shit
Shul: synagogue or school
Shvitzing: sweating

Treif: unkosher
Tuchus: buttocks
Tummler: comic entertainer
Verklempt: choked up
Yagde: blueberries
Yenta: busybody, gossip

A Short History of the Golden Era of the Catskills, known as the Borscht Belt

The 1940s-1960s marked the glory days of the Catskill Mountains hotel industry. Hundreds of hotels and resorts thrived in the area.

Top-level entertainers and comedians of the time took to the stages. The guests were predominantly Jewish, banned at many other resorts but welcomed in the mountains. The staff comprised immigrants, refugees, and people seeking the American Dream.

Bungalow colonies also flourished in the towns of Sullivan and Ulster counties, along with summer camps. The peak came in the mid-1950s. Then, three A's changed everything: Air conditioning, Assimilation, and Airplanes.

Members of the crime syndicate group Murder, Inc. often visited the mountains. Although their reign only lasted from the late '20s to the early '40s. There may still be bodies buried in the Catskill Mountains. This is where our story continues.

SUMMER 1954

The moon was a crescent, casting long shadows that slithered through the forest clearing. She knelt and touched the earth. The topsoil contained bone fragments. The gentleness of the wind rustling the trees offered a stark contrast to the churning in her stomach. She started to dig...

PART I
1954

Chapter 1

DOTTY

"Every hotel claims to have the best facilities and the greatest rates," Dotty told Eva, pointing to the *New York Times* travel section covered in advertisements encouraging guests to come to the mountains.

Eva placed a bowl of chopped liver with thin slices of rye bread on the card table. "The Concord is number one."

Wholeheartedly agreeing, Dotty settled into her seat next to the hosta garden and pulled out her official 1954 National Mah Jongg League card. Together, the dear friends removed the three sets of suits called Bams, Cracks, and Dots from the carrier. Two other waitresses were expected to join them for their weekly game.

After her two children were born, Dotty no longer worked weekday meals. She had been a waitress at the renowned Concord Hotel ever since graduating high school in the Bronx. By chance, she was assigned Eva as her roommate. It was that same year, 1944, that she learned to play Mah Jongg.

1944 brought a lot of memories to the forefront. That was when, in the middle of the Danny Kaye show, Irving Cohen, the head maître d' at the hotel, had fired them. Thankfully, he had needed their help so desperately that he had rescinded all their terminations immediately. Dotty shook thoughts of that night away—she did not like to think of the gangster who kidnapped them, driving them to Rochester, trapping them in the cubbyhole, and then what followed.

Eva went back inside, and Dotty picked up the

latest issue of the local *Republican Watchman* newspaper. A headline caught her attention as she was flipping through.

Locked Door at the Courthouse Raises Questions

She touched her above-shoulder-length, dishwater-blonde hair while continuing to read about the electrician asking for permission to remove the locks.

Eva peeked over her shoulder. "What could they be hiding in there?"

Always intrigued by a good mystery, Dotty made a note to watch for updates on the story as it progressed.

"I forgot to make the natural soda pop. Come, there's time to pick fresh *yagdas*." Eva was carrying a bottle of seltzer in one hand and a pitcher and a wooden spoon in the other.

Dotty closed the newspaper and looked across the street, her view of the blueberry bushes in the field obscured by Eva's white Chevrolet parked under her carport. "Mrs. Steingold warned you to stay away."

Eva rolled her eyes. "Come, we don't have much time." She began crossing the street, her chestnut-colored curls speckled with sunbeams.

Hershel, the talent booker at the Concord, known as "the Casanova of the Concord," was driving up the hill in a black Cadillac Eldorado. "Hello!" he shouted.

Dotty waved while Eva twisted her face into a sneer.

"I have news," Hershel hollered, idling in his Caddy.

"Well, spit it out already," said Eva.

"I'm going to work at the Laurels!"

"Why would you want to do that?" asked Eva.

"I'm ready for a change."

"Oh, admit it, you just want to go to where the young singles are," Eva spat.

Hershel smirked. "Think what you may."

The Laurels had a reputation as the place to go if you wanted to see the sunrise over Sackett Lake. It was not uncommon for the 1,000-seat nightclub to still be bustling at the crack of dawn. Popular comedians would show up unannounced and leave the guests clutching their stomachs.

"Have you told Arthur yet?" Dotty asked, swallowing hard. She did not like the idea of leaving Arthur in the lurch during the busiest season.

Arthur Winarick, the owner of the Concord Hotel, was a successful businessman. Before becoming a hotelier, he was a barber with access to alcohol due to his profession. It was the Prohibition era when he and his chemist brother partnered to launch Jeris Hair Tonic. Bootleg liquor was how he made his fortune. When Grossinger's, the most lavish hotel at the time, turned him away, he vowed to create the largest hotel in the mountains. He accomplished that with the Concord, purchasing concrete and steel structures from the 1939 World's Fair. He also dismantled a ferryboat he had bought for the steel.

"I'm headed to meet with him now." Hershel waved a hand in the air and revved his engine.

"If I had chosen to stay with him, my life would have been one tumultuous act after the next." They watched him disappear up the hill and around the bend.

There was no way Dotty was going to argue against that. She had been pleased when Eva and Leon became a solid couple. Leon was Abe's co-captain in the staff dining room. He was a refugee from Poland. Eva was a refugee from Austria.

In her gingham pedal pushers, Dotty squatted down beside a patch of blueberry bushes.

"There's nothing more delightful than a *yagde* warmed by the sun," Eva repeated what she said every single time.

Dotty bit down on a tart-tasting blueberry as a robust middle-aged woman was coming straight at them with a gardening hoe in hand.

Eva blew air out of her lips before saying, "Hello, Mrs. Steingold."

"Stay away from my *yagde* bushes!" shouted a furious Mrs. Steingold.

Dotty jumped up. Every summer, they picked fruit from their former landlord's property, but Mrs. Steingold had been prickly about it ever since they had built their own houses.

"I know all about Bill's card den he's running from one of my bungalows." Mrs. Steingold was shaking her gardening hoe in the air.

Dotty had yet to visit the bungalow that Bill Graham turned into 'the spot to play cards for the summer,' but she did know that Eva was a regular. Eva was the queen of card games in the region.

"Nobody is getting hurt; we are just having fun," Eva snickered, yanking a plump blueberry from a branch.

"I'm kicking Bill out this weekend—that's all he paid me through. I want him gone." Mrs. Steingold cursed in Yiddish. "*Makhasheyfe! Dummkopf.*"

"Bill was a 'One Thousand Children' survivor," Eva reminded her.

Dotty thought it was extraordinary that Bill was one of the children rescued from the Nazis in Europe and brought to the United States as an orphan. She knew he had been awarded a Bronze Star and a Purple Heart for serving in the Korean War and had an aspiration of being a concert promoter. She, like everyone else, could tell he was going to make a name for himself. And she knew Mrs. Steingold was stuck with him for the summer; she would not actually toss him to the curb.

Mrs. Steingold started dredging up old hostility. "Your husbands promised not to design rentals in your houses. That's the only reason I agreed to sell the land to them."

"Why should you tell us what to do in our own homes? There are lots of workers who need places to live—none of us will have vacancies," said Eva.

Dotty stared at the main building to the right of her. As newlyweds, following an enchanting wedding in the Bronx, she and Abe had rented an apartment inside the property that was a farm and boarding house when Mr. and Mrs. Steingold had purchased it. The Steingolds had the vision of splitting up the building, converting it into five apartments. It was a hoppin' place. Eva and Leon had also lived there.

Once Al, named after Abe's brother who had been killed in the war, was born, Dotty and Abe moved into a bungalow situated on the Steingolds' property. The Steingolds had also owned several acres across the street, which were originally a chicken farm. It took a couple of rounds of negotiations, and the Steingolds agreed to sell them land to build their own homes.

Eva had her hands on her hips in a standoff with Mrs. Steingold. "I'll plant *yagde* bushes in my backyard."

Dotty did not understand why Mrs. Steingold was against them being landlords. Many hotel workers needed housing, and her properties were never vacant; they were not stealing competition away.

She and Abe had hired an in-demand architect to design rentals in the basement of their new brown-painted, butterfly-roofed house, and by word of mouth, they had quickly filled both. A busboy and a waitress currently rented from them. The bedroom they built off the billiard room was where their live-in maid, Clem, stayed.

Eva and Leon also had rentals in their basement, and Irving's house had been designed with a rental apartment in the back. The man who owned the laundromat at the Concord lived there.

"The money is simply too good to pass up. It's an extra income. We can declare the rental space on our taxes as a business expense. Mrs. Steingold, you will have to deal with it," Eva said matter-of-factly.

Mrs. Steingold turned and locked eyes with Dotty. "How'd you like to be my assistant den mother, with the idea that you'll become the den mother of Cub Scouts after I hand over the torch next year?"

"Are you retiring?" Dotty asked, slack-jawed. Mrs. Steingold had led the Cub Scouts since her son had joined, and he was now pushing thirty. Countless Cub Scouts had earned adventure badges because they had spent one day a week with Mrs. Steingold for five years of their young lives.

Mrs. Steingold let the gardening hoe fall to her side. "It's time. My knees aren't getting any younger."

"I'd be honored." Dotty was already imagining

herself decked out in a khaki button-down top paired with an army green skirt.

A dry coughing sound escaped Eva's lips.

"Very good. I'll see you on Thursday at my house for your first meeting as my assistant." Mrs. Steingold pulled a garden fork out of her gardening tool belt.

Eva dropped the wooden spoon into the pitcher and scowled.

"*Oy vey.*" Both of their sons were five years old, born four months apart. Although not willing to forfeit the position, Dotty certainly was not thrilled about being on Eva's bad side.

Achoo. Boychik, the small gray cat with black stripes, must be nearby. A senior kitty now, he no longer called the nightclub at the Concord his home; instead, he roamed the neighborhood and claimed Eva's porch as his favorite spot. He spent his days lounging and receiving attention from all the children. Occasionally, he still ventured up to the hotel. It was Leon who loved him the most.

Boychik gingerly walked toward her; he spit a piece of torn emerald-green fabric with sequins out of his mouth. Everything started to spin as she snatched the material off the grass. It matched the same material and color as the floor-length gown she had worn in 1944 when she was kidnapped.

CHAPTER 2

ABE

"Psst, Abey. I've got news." All six feet two inches of Hershel sprang from around a corner as Abe walked down the hallway toward the staff dining room.

"Tell me."

"I'm booking the talent at the Laurels from now on!"

Eyes wide, mouth agape, Abe said, "You really are leaving the Concord?"

With pushed-back shoulders, Hershel nodded.

"Well, why do you want to do that?"

"My seven-year itch expired a while ago."

Abe was happy for his pal and playfully punched his arm. "We will miss you around here."

"You'll come to visit. The pageant is coming up." Hershel winked. "They are crowning a new Miss Laurels. The contestants are guests, and the judges are, too."

Abe checked his watch. He needed to help Leon set up for dinner.

"Go," said Hershel. "I'll catch up with you later."

Leon skidded to Abe's side as soon as he entered the staff dining room. His hands were full of coleslaw and lemon slices—the livestock. That was the term for all the perishable food that the whole table shared. "The haddock is tasty tonight."

He would suggest that option to the undecisive diner. Unable to remain tight-lipped, he blurted out, "Hershel is switching to the Laurels."

Leon scoffed. "I won't lose any sleep over that."

The two co-captains flew through setup.

"Here's the man who never has to worry about 'the Concord Syndrome.'" Abe greeted Buddy Hackett, using the term to describe when guests vacate their seats early, bragging about fleeing a free show and complaining about the lousy act. He led the "King of the Concord" to his designated table.

"Everyone wants to be here. Saying you closed a show at the Concord is great advertising. Where are all the movers and shakers tonight?" asked Buddy with a contagious, upbeat attitude.

"I'm looking at one." Abe tilted the water pitcher, filling Buddy's glass.

Buddy was a frequent diner in the staff dining room. Arthur Winarick held a year-round room for him. The guests loved him, and everyone at the Concord took good care of him.

Buddy remained jolly. "Sid will be here on Saturday. He probably won't make it until lunchtime. He just wrapped up *Your Show of Shows*, and he's squeezing the Concord in before *Caesar's Hour* begins."

Abe knew that Sid Caesar was on hiatus and that the two celebrated actors and comedians were good friends.

"Duke Ellington will be here next week. Billy Eckstine is coming back the following week. It's nonstop, first-rate entertainment up here these days," Leon added.

"Duke's a gargantuan eater, especially dessert. And Billy's as smooth as they come." Abe could confirm this to be true, having served the talented entertainers their meals in the staff dining room on their previous visits. Billy Eckstine, a jazz singer and bandleader, had been the first Black headliner at the Concord in 1949.

Buddy raised his glass in the air. "Keep them well-fed, Abey. Serve them the best *milkhik* and *fleishig* they've ever tasted."

"You know I always do." Even entertainers who were not Jewish or did not keep kosher at home ate their meals on separate plates at the Concord—one set was for meat, the other for dairy.

Jimmy Demaret, the golf pro, entered the staff dining room and went directly to the 4-top table where he ate on every occasion.

Irving showed up with a pink bundle in his arms. "This little one is the result of my matchmaking skills."

Abe smiled at the tiny ankle-biter. "Time flies." He was thinking about how fast his own children were growing up. Al, whose namesake was Abe's older brother who had died during World War II, was five years old. Linda had recently turned four years old.

Abe pictured the pegboard system Irving displayed in his office. The pink pegs represented the women, and the blue pegs represented the men. He kept track of ages and whether they were single or married by lighter or darker shading. That way he would sit nice, single, Jewish girls next to nice, single, Jewish boys. The system had earned him the nickname "King Cupid."

"It's hard to believe it's been a decade since you two started as co-captains," Irving said to Abe and Leon after he handed the baby back to its parents.

Abe's mind flitted to a decade ago and their

abrupt firing. In an unfortunate turn of events, they had become mixed up with Murder, Inc.

Jacob "Jack" Drucker was a local Hurleyville farm boy turned gangster. He oversaw the Sullivan County arm of the crime syndicate Murder, Inc. Hershel, who was now one of Abe's best pals, and Drucker's family had farms bordering each other. Hershel's brothers currently ran the farm; Hershel was just a silent partner. When Drucker was arrested for the death of another gangster, Walter Sage, he asked Hershel to hide his fortune of "bootleg bounty" from law enforcement. Hershel did, and a whole slew of events were set into motion.

An associate of Drucker's nicknamed D.R., short for Drucker's Rat, claimed the money was owed to him. D.R. ended up kidnapping Dotty and Abe. Then D.R. was killed right when they were rescued by Sy, a man to whom they had grown close. Sy was not a gangster; he was a cop whose badge was revoked because he leaned on the side of tough punishment for bad guys.

Luckily, Irving had hired them right back. He needed them to serve breakfast, and they had stayed out of trouble from that time onward.

Abe agreed that it was hard to believe that ten years had gone by so quickly. Once upon a time, they had each been a busboy in the main dining room. They had also married, built families, and reported to the staff dining room every single day.

Zero Mostel made his appearance. "You'll be eating right over here," Abe told the well-liked actor, singer, and comedian, ushering him to his own table. His style of eating was so sloppy that it was a necessity. Fortunately, there was no dress code inside the staff dining room, or Zero would have been turned away.

Zero took a seat at a table by himself. He was singing a jingle, "Abey, bring me another chicken."

Abe's eyes crinkled, always enjoying Zero Mostel's visits at the Concord. So did the guests. Little Al had seen Zero perform his act where he turned into a teapot, using his facial muscles in excess, and still laughed at it. Zero had been blacklisted by Hollywood for being a member of the Communist Party, but the mountains accepted him.

Mr. Pierpont, the fencing instructor, ordered his herring salad in a mix of broken English and his native French. Abe had learned a little French in high school back in Brighton Beach, enough that he was able to carry on a primitive conversation.

"Your son should take lessons from me."

He did not think Dotty would approve of it until Al was older. He nodded his head at the suggestion anyway.

Sherry Dubois, the masterful mambo instructor at the Concord, breezed through the door. Buddy set his eggplant spread on pumpernickel aside and stopped bantering with his seatmates to greet his fiancée.

Abe had not known Buddy as a *tummler* over at the Golden Hotel when he was first starting out. He had heard enough stories about his time there, cracking jokes and dancing with older ladies that he could easily envision a school-aged Buddy charming everyone he had encountered.

Zero Mostel tossed the chicken bone that he had been sucking on aside. He called for a cold cup of *schav,* so Abe hustled away.

"Where's my friend Hershel?" asked Buddy as Leon was filling his water glass.

Leon wrinkled his nose.

The talent booker usually stopped by at mealtimes to say hi to the entertainers on-site, so Abe figured Hershel must be busy announcing his Laurels news. He held the *schav* and a plate of blintzes, recalling when Leon was a busboy and met the stunning waitress Eva in the dining room. He was glad the two of them had ended up together. Back then, Abe and Leon were roommates.

Zero's table for one was already hidden beneath dirty saucers and monkey dishes. Abe handed Zero the soup along with a clean napkin for the soup that would be dripping down his chin any moment.

The dining room cleared, and the co-captains counted quarters. It was a system they had created because they felt they deserved tips like the waiters in the main dining room. Every person who ate in the staff dining room now left a tip in the form of a quarter after their meal.

Abe turned to Leon. "Say, let's go over to Kutsher's Thursday night. The mountain basketball game will be held there. We'll get a good look at that high school player, Wilt Chamberlain."

"I'd fancy setting eyes on Wilt. I heard he's so lanky that he simply stands outside and lifts guests' luggage through second-floor windows. Imagine having him as your bellhop!"

"We can't expect Wilt to be working at Kutsher's for long, not with the praise and potential we've been hearing about Wilt 'the Stilt.' Red Auerbach is back over at Kutsher's coaching professional basketball players for the summer against other hotels. We'll get a good look at him as well." Abe dragged a chair across the room and flicked off the lights. It would be his first time laying eyes on the Boston Celtics' coach, Red, who spent his summers in the Catskills. He stepped into the hallway, and a long, thin shadow slipped away.

Chapter 3

"Come on, Al. It's time to go to Cub Scouts," Dotty hollered on Thursday, sporting her new khaki button-down top paired with an army green skirt. Her heart melted at seeing Al in his own little brown uniform.

"What badge are we working on today?" Al swung an empty copper bucket into the air.

"The Lion Badge. There are six activities required to earn your badge, and you've only completed two so far."

"I really want the Lion Badge! Where's David?"

She saw Eva nurturing her perennials and instinctively waved. Eva ripped a weed out of the ground. Dotty sighed and put her hand on the small of Al's back, leading him across the street.

Achoo. Boychik strolled to the blueberry bushes, with his tail swaying. "Did you bring me any more surprises today?" she whispered his way. She had convinced herself the piece of emerald-green fabric was something the laundry man who lived at Irving's must have dropped. It was pure coincidence that it reminded her of the evening gown given to Abe by Moss Hart, the playwright.

Mrs. Steingold handed Dotty a piece of paper. It said that the group was working on the Mountain Lion part of the Lion Badge. Today they would learn about the buddy system when going on an adventure. Only seven of the eight kids were in attendance. That meant one boy would not have a buddy. Dotty sighed again.

As they were spraying the boys with bug repellent, Leon showed up with David by his side. "Why should he miss out? Eva is the one who is acting self-centered, always having to be the star. Let David enjoy Cub Scouts. Dotty, I'm sure you are making a fine assistant den mother." He tugged at the rim of his newsboy cap and strode off.

Al and the rest of the boys were happy to see their pal keep his perfect attendance record intact. There was a lot of excitement in the air to earn the Lion Badges. Dotty spied Eva under a birch tree at the edge of her property. She waved, but to no surprise, she was met with the sight of Eva's backside turned toward her.

The hour was over in a blink. A reporter from the *Republican Watchman* stopped by to jot down Dotty's name and snap a photo of the entire troop. Mrs. Steingold stood in the center, her arms around the two boys closest to her. The news of her retirement would be announced in the next issue.

Dotty turned toward the birch tree, but Eva was nowhere in sight. She could only imagine how much Eva's jealousy would skyrocket once the article was published.

The meeting wrapped up, and nobody came to pick up David. Al and David raced each other across the street. They found Eva with curlers in her hair, holding a green watering can in one hand and a Lucky Strike in the other. David dumped his bucket at Eva's feet, proud to show her the feathers, sticks, leaves, and flowers he had collected.

Eva picked up the drooping daisy, ignoring Dotty until she spun around and spat, "I thought Mrs. Steingold would be teaching the children how to be an *alte makh sheyfe.*"

Not willing to squabble, Dotty kept her mouth shut and went home to change out of her uniform. She ripped open an envelope from the IRS that looked rather important and hustled right back out the side door. "I've been audited. The government found out I haven't been reporting all my tips!" *Achoo.*

"I guess you will go to jail."

"Jail!" she gasped. "I'm not doing anything that all the rest of you aren't doing." Dotty and Abe had been stuffing cash into a metal safe in their bedroom and not reporting it, just as their friends had done. *Achoo.*

Eva poured the remaining water from the watering can onto a bed of marigolds while Dotty clutched the paper and considered getting in touch with a lawyer right away.

Leon came strutting up the driveway. His whistling halted when he saw Dotty's ashen face.

Eva set the watering can down with a thud. "I need to remove my curlers. There's a poker game." She stared at the bungalow dubbed Bill's card den across the street, then simply turned around and shut the front door behind her.

"I'm sorry she's holding a grudge. Is there anything I can help you with?" Leon was eyeing the envelope in her hand.

Dotty handed over the letter and removed a Lucky Strike from the brand-new pack she had in her pocket.

"It's not so bad; you have to pay a fine. Go over to the courthouse."

"Why should they have to know every penny we make? Abe and I pay our taxes diligently." Dotty blew a plume of smoke out of her lips.

"Who reports all their income?" Leon shrugged a shoulder as Boychik nuzzled against his legs. He bent down and scratched the cat's neck.

Leon was the straightest arrow of them all, so if he was not reporting his tips, she supposed it must not be the most heinous thing ever. "I guess we'll have to start doing things by the book." *Achoo.*

"Let's hope nobody else is audited." Leon tapped Boychik on the nose.

Back at home, she stuffed the letter into a drawer, deciding it was finally time to learn to play tennis and marched herself up to the courts at the Concord.

CHAPTER 4

ABE

Jimmy Demaret was the first to arrive for dinner on Thursday evening. "Did you hear Grossinger's will have man-made snow next winter?"

Abe pulled out the golf pro's seat. "Arthur must be having a fit that he didn't think of it first."

"I bet he'll have Raymond make bigger and better man-made snow now. Adding air conditioning throughout the Concord was his last big project. He should be ready to tackle another one." Leon joined the conversation. Raymond Parker had married Winarick's daughter, Clara, and now held the reins of the day-to-day management.

Dinner was a breeze. They cleared livestock, wiped down tables, then tore off their aprons with gusto. Once they reached Kutsher's, Red Auerbach was flailing his arms around, yelling a call out to seven-foot-one Wilt Chamberlain, who was dribbling the basketball down the court. Abe's eyes bugged out when he saw Wilt simply toss the ball through the hoop. Wild cheers filled the evening air as an energized crowd hooted and hollered.

"Milton Kutsher and the mountains won the jackpot by acquiring such a coach. Red's growing fame helped turn Kutsher's into a powerhouse for basketball up here," Leon said with his face close to Abe's right ear.

Abe stared across the street at the large, yellow, brightly lit, welcoming Kutsher's sign that sat atop the ritzy hotel. Six-foot-seven Joe Holup, a star at George Washington University, was playing on the opposing team for the Nevele Hotel. He was scoring bucket after bucket.

"Don't let him dominate the game! He's wheeling and dealing all over you!" Red yelled at Wilt, kicking the ground and jerking his thumb at the sidelines.

Wilt huffed back in frustration.

Hard focused on the action, standing near the home team's hoop, was the owner of Kutsher's Country Club. Milton Kutsher was connected with the athletic world, and because of that, his hotel was known for sports. He was also a trustee of the recently founded National Basketball Association Hall of Fame in Springfield, Massachusetts.

Abe puffed out his chest; to witness a game while out in the country with such high-profile names was special. "Wish we could place a bet like the good ol' days."

Leon was giving him the side eye. "Sy's lucky the feds didn't bring him in last time for bankrolling the operation."

Abe raked his left hand through his hair, remembering the colossal college basketball point-shaving scandal. The investment club that Sy had invited him to join a decade ago had disbanded after Sy moved to Atlantic City. "I'm surprised at the number of players who owned up to fixing games, but I guess I'd come clean if faced with time in the slammer."

"A $600 bribe to control the points of a game is what brought it all down."

"It was fun while it lasted."

The best players in the country had been recruited to the mountains for "summer jobs." In reality, they were there to entertain the guests and throw games accordingly. The corruption crumbled once the authorities got wind—legacies of coaches were ruined, college careers tarnished, and players who had a future in professional basketball were banned from ever joining the NBA.

"Look!" gasped Leon.

Abe whipped his head around to the other side of the court, flabbergasted to be staring at one of the best heavyweight boxers in the world. Ezzard Charles threw fake punches at the crowd. "Did you hear Irving say Rocky Marciano is back over at Grossinger's training for their fight?"

"There's a big heavyweight championship on the line; I'd surely hope both boxers are practicing with all their might."

"I'm putting my money on Marciano this time." Abe stuck out his hand to shake on it.

"Ezzard." Leon returned a firm handshake.

Wilt's fallaway jumper went right through the hoop. "No kidding, Milton recruited him here as a bellhop." Abe watched the star player run off the court with a towel draped over his head.

"He didn't make as many baskets as I expected until the end of the first half."

Abe said, "Oh, he'll bounce back." And that is exactly what he did. Wilt "the Stilt" dominated the second half, and Kutsher's won the game.

"Do you ever think about working at a smaller hotel?" Leon asked as Abe drove his mint-green Chrysler Windsor in the direction of Kiamesha Lake.

"Why would I want to leave the Concord?" Abe slowed down as they drove by the new bar that had recently been built five hundred feet across from the Concord. The sign that had gone up introducing the name to the world was sleek and inviting. The Rib Room & Pussy Cat Lounge would give the staff a place to go and let loose without staying on hotel grounds. "Let's go in for a nightcap," he suggested.

"All right, but just one," Leon said hesitantly.

The jukebox was blasting "Dream Baby" by Roy Orbison, a cloud of smoke hung heavy, and there was a serious game of pool happening in the corner.

Leon used the washroom while Abe chose a bar stool and ordered himself a scotch neat and Leon a scotch on the rocks. Abe took a healthy gulp from his glass and heard a thud as the door slammed open.

A voice he recognized shouted out, "Let's party!"

Abe spun around.

"Abey!" yelled Hershel, slapping him on the back. "You ordered me a drink." Hershel finished the scotch meant for Leon in two big swallows and hopped onto the next barstool.

Leon jabbed his thumb into Hershel's shoulder. "You are in my seat."

Hershel did not budge. Instead, he flagged down the bartender.

Leon crossed his arms and huffed.

Abe shook his head back and forth, wishing that his two best pals could bury the hatchet for good; being caught in the middle was no fun.

"You already stole my *bashert* from me. What more do you want?" Hershel kept his back to Leon.

"I'll walk home," Leon said.

Abe slid off his barstool.

"Abey Baby, don't go," Hershel begged.

Leon was bent down on the curb outside. He picked up a photograph that Boychik had carried over and thrust it at Abe. "It's some old, weathered house."

Abe stumbled on his feet. *Why in the world did Boychik have a picture of the creepy house in Rochester?*

CHAPTER 5

DOTTY

"We practiced my backhand," Dotty told Abe on Friday morning as she folded the crocheted blanket into a neat pile. She had fallen asleep on the couch while watching *The Bob Hope Show* the night before.

"I'm glad you enjoyed your first tennis lesson, Dot." He blew on his mug of coffee.

"I went ahead and signed up for weekly lessons. It'll help me stay trim." Now that the kids were 4 and 5, she was able to focus on her hobbies again.

"Don't expect to see too much of me, and don't expect me to get much sleep either. The hotel will be a circus."

She returned his smile while shimmying her shoulders, excited about full pockets after the busy weekend. "Oh, what a show it's going to be inside the Cordillion Room tomorrow with the premiere of *Saturday Night at the Concord Hotel with Sid Caesar, Buddy Hackett, Sherry Dubois, and the Mambo Team.*"

He put his half-empty mug in the sink. "The talent lined up is impressive. Tips should be very good in the main dining room."

I'm heading over to the courthouse this morning," she reminded him.

"Do you need money for the fine?" He was already removing cash from his wallet.

She tucked the cash into her purse and listened to the door clank shut behind him. Then she turned to the newspaper. Reading about permission given to the electrician to break all locks at the courthouse to access the hidden room piqued her curiosity. She raised an eyebrow. Would she witness any of the activity when she went to the courthouse in an hour?

Hershel hollered through the doorway. "Abey, are you home?"

"He's already up at the hotel." She lifted her mug in the air. "Care for any?"

Hershel shook his mop of black hair. "No," he said, gazing through the kitchen window at Eva watering her marigolds. "She has the most beautiful flowers."

"She waters them every day at this time." Dotty did not disclose that she and Eva were currently at odds.

A faraway look crossed his face. "She deserved someone without blood on his hands."

Dotty thought Leon was the more stable choice for Eva to have chosen as a partner, but she had hoped they could all be friends again. *Why would he say he had blood on his hands?* Hershel was no murderer. It was true he used to get mixed up in no-good situations, but for the last decade, he had kept himself out of trouble—for the most part.

Dismissing his statement as nonsense, she reasoned it must be a metaphor. She went to apply lipstick and spritzed herself with Chantilly perfume before driving over to the Monticello courthouse. The fragrant notes of orange blossoms and lemon lifted her mood.

***

"Where do I go?" she asked the first person she encountered when walking through the entrance, holding the IRS letter in her hand.

"Go to the clerk, right over there," said the man

who wore a black patch over one eye.

Dotty stood in line. There were two other people in front of her. She peered around, not seeing anyone who resembled an electrician about to start breaking locks.

"Hello," she said to the clerk when it was her turn.

"How can I help you?" The clerk was mousy in appearance and so petite that she used a cushion on top of the stool she sat on to be closer to eye level with the person she was helping.

"I have this letter."

The clerk's complexion became pale as she read it. "Excuse me," she said.

Dotty stood, drumming her fingertips on the counter. Shabbat dinner at the Concord was on deck.

The clerk returned. "I'm sorry, I got thirsty for a glass of water. Did you bring the money to pay the fine with you?" Her face looked feverish.

What frightened her? Dotty removed cash from her purse.

The clerk wrote out a receipt and handed it over with a tremble in her hands. "You are all set."

CHAPTER 6

ABE

Friday night had been one of the busiest he had experienced, and Saturday was following in its footsteps. Abe placed a plate of gefilte fish in front of Irving at his 4-top. Across from Irving sat Sholom Secunda, the musical director hired after Alexander Olshanetsky's sudden death at the age of 54 in 1946. Sholom was known for his hit "Bei Mir Bistu Shein" in the 1930s. He led a 65-piece orchestra on Thursday evenings, and on the weekends, his concerts showcased Cantor Richard Tucker. Sholom also conducted High Holy Day services at the hotel.

Irving carried on, red-faced. "A secret ballot has been cast among employees. Now a union is coming to the Concord by a five to one vote."

Leon whispered in Abe's ear, "The agreement is that employees will have a defined workweek, receive regular wage increases, and be given medical coverage. It doesn't sound so bad to me to have seniority and job security."

Abe thought back to when he had tricked Leon into attending the union meeting with Dotty. They had both been hankering to land the one waiter position that was open at the time. Irving had been enraged when Dotty and Leon had shown up at the meeting. Abe had felt guilty for his part.

Now Abe hoped Leon would hush up. Nonetheless, he continued to whisper, "No longer can bosses fire anyone just because they want to replace them with a 'political' of their choosing." Politicals was the name given to friends or family members of the higher-ups.

Onto a new topic, Irving lowered his voice and flagged over Leon. "You're both invited to a private meeting in the back room on Monday. It'll be between breakfast and lunch. Dress sharply."

Abe held his head high and scooted over to Boris Shalman, who did all the electrical work at the hotel. He was taking his time deciding between a cold tuna fish or a hot fish Cantonese.

The staff dining room was boisterous, with one person after the next stopping by to eat their dinner, leaving no time until clean-up for the two co-captains to discuss the flattering invitation.

"I know you can't wait to tell Eva we received a personal invite to the back room," Abe said as he pushed a 4-top into a corner.

Leon's shoulders drooped. "Eva's had a heavy enough hand in gambling lately."

Abe narrowed his eyes, catching the unpleasant tone in Leon's voice. Eva and Leon had always been a solid pair. He crossed his fingers that Buddy's act would hit it out of the park and leave them chuckling so hard that all their worries would disappear.

The last chair was pushed in, and Leon flicked off the lights. Then they departed for the Cordillion Room, built to replace the Rio Cabana. The original nightclub burned to the ground when D.R.'s mother tried to feed the stray cats on the Concord grounds. She dropped the match, and that was the end.

Sherry Dubois was hovering in front of the grandiose red curtains on the circular stage. Abe saved a spot for Dotty in the standing space beside him. Leon gestured to the closest cocktail waitress and ordered a scotch on the rocks.

Right before the lights went dark, Dotty slithered to Abe's side, wearing her white uniform and looking flushed from serving a hectic Saturday night dinner. "Eva isn't with you?"

Dotty gave him a pinched smile and shook her head "no."

When Leon learned that his wife was missing the big show, he ordered another scotch. Abe wanted to tell Dotty about his special invitation from Irving, but the lights were lowered. He would have to fill her in later.

Sherry Dubois and the Mambo Team had the room hanging on to every kick and flick of their feet as they playfully danced onstage. Buddy and Sid made the crowd roar. Everyone's spirits were soaring over the top-notch entertainment. Guests were ready to brag to their friends about it.

"What's 'the Concord Syndrome?'" Dotty said, her eyes twinkling from watching the impressive show. She yawned. "I'm going home. Enjoy the fight."

Abe stepped forward and kissed her goodbye, eager to listen to Rocky Marciano and Ezzard Charles exchanging punches on the radio. The fight was taking place at Yankee Stadium.

Abe and Leon's next stop was the Night Owl. It was packed with people huddled around the radio, which was broadcasting the fight. Leon promptly ordered another scotch on the rocks and leaned against a high-top table. He was standing between two off-duty lobby porters. Abe ordered himself a scotch neat and joined them.

"Jennie Grossinger must be tickled pink that Marciano has The G's name stitched inside his robe," said the day porter.

"Milton Blackstone is a marketing genius, I tell you. The way he invited Barney Ross to train, free of charge, at the G in the '30s. It used to be mostly wannabes and a few soon-to-bes coming up to the mountains, and now all the professional boxers want to hone their craft at the most popular resorts," said the other porter.

Milton Blackstone was the PR guy who booked the talent over at Grossinger's. Aware that the deep competition between Hershel and Milton Blackstone was personal, Abe was glad that Hershel was not nearby.

The bartender increased the volume on the radio. "Charles takes a right uppercut to the head. Marciano counters with a hard left hook to the chin. A solid right to the jaw by Marciano. Charles puts out a jab, puts out another. Charles takes a right hand to the body. Less than two minutes left in the last round. Marciano is tired; he's hanging on. Marciano's face is a bloody mess. It's all over; they've thrown their arms around each other!" shouted the commentator.

"Tell us who won!" Abe yelled at the radio.

On cue, the commentator announced, "decision favors Marciano."

Leon reached for his wallet, and Abe tucked his winnings into his pocket. The band was about to go on, and the bar was rowdy. Leon settled onto a stool. Abe raised his eyebrows. It was unlike his pal to go on a bender.

Abe partook in one final round of scotch neat and

encouraged Leon to call it a night. When two women tried to block their exit, Abe thought it completely out of character for Leon to maintain prolonged eye contact and compliment their mink stoles. He shoved his pal outside and dropped him off at his doorstep. "Take an aspirin," he warned, not wanting Leon to show up to work hungover with a headache in the morning.

Abe kept his eyes on Leon, lingering beside Eva's rose bushes until the party line rang. His neighbors shared the phone line with them; he tapped his foot, listening to see if anyone else answered.

"Abe-*ala*."

"Hello, Ma." He shook his head; it was late, and dealing with his mother right now would take more energy than he had reserved.

"Jean has met a fella named Joseph on the Brooklyn Trolley."

"Well, that sounds swell. I'll invite them to visit soon." He was smiling into the phone, thinking of his younger sister.

Ma barked, "I'm *verklempt*. Joseph is not Jewish."

"Surely he'll only be a fling." Abe chewed on his thumbnail. *How is Papa dealing with this news?*

Papa had been a rabbi back in Ukraine, but in the United States, he never had the chance to continue his rabbinic studies. Leading his own congregation was never in the cards again. He had to settle for pushing a peddler's cart and selling bananas.

"I miss Al." Ma was now wailing. She was belligerent, as she usually was about everything. His parents were divorced; both had remarried.

Abe also missed his eldest brother, who had died

when a Japanese sniper shot him while he was setting up communications on one of the Pacific islands. Al had been their leader and protector as the siblings moved through foster care.

"Norman's pursuing another master's degree in English at Columbia University. He's also teaching literature to high schoolers." Abe clucked his tongue, purposely switching to a more pleasant topic. In awe of how his younger brother did all his studying on nights and weekends, his heart swelled with pride over Norman's accomplishments.

"You were always the most athletic one, beating everyone at stickball, but Norman is the smartest one."

Abe took a heavy inhalation. Ma's insults carried a punch. She was still spewing on, but he hung up anyway. *Click.* Then he checked outside to make sure Leon was not stuck in a rose bush.

The photograph of the house that Boychik had somehow found had been pushed to the back burner due to the busy weekend. He removed it from inside an encyclopedia and stared at it. It would scare Dotty, so he had kept it hidden.

CHAPTER 7

DOTTY

While setting out silverware for breakfast, Eva hurled a copy of the *Republican Watchman* at her. They were both wearing their yellow uniforms, required for breakfast and lunch, the two dairy meals of the day.

Dotty studied the black-and-white photograph on the third page. Then she read the adjacent paragraph that announced Mrs. Steingold was retiring and she was the new assistant den mother. It also told how the boys were working on earning their Lion Badges. Proud of the recognition in the local newspaper, her lips curled into a smile.

Eva stomped away. With pep in her step, Dotty folded the newspaper and put it on the server stand. Breakfast begged for her attention. The guests were in pleasant moods, and she was in fine spirits. Apple griddle cakes were the popular item of the morning.

Eva and the waiter, Bill Graham, rushed out the door before Dotty's stations were bare of tablecloths. Irving did not notice because he was *schmoozing* with a VIP couple who had driven up for the day.

"I heard you're handed a pastrami sandwich with cream soda upon arrival at Bill's card den, and nobody has to pay a penny for it," said Dotty's busboy, now removing the tablecloth.

She pictured the bungalow at the Steingolds' packed with people playing cards and Mrs. Steingold shaking her gardening hoe at the door. "Irving is furious with Bill for smuggling food out of the hotel.

Were you here last Friday night when he erupted like a volcano after catching a cook attempting to hide food under his jacket to sneak off to Bill's?"

The busboy grew serious. "Eva better be careful. I also heard a chef lost all his earnings for an entire season in one night inside Bill's card den."

"Where did Bill and Eva go?" Irving growled, walking up behind her.

Dotty hopped a foot into the air. She grabbed the dirty tablecloth out of her busboy's arms and skedaddled to the laundry room. She knew the bad blood between Bill and their boss ran deep. Bill backed a union coming to the Concord. Irving did not.

CHAPTER 8

ABE

"I saw your wife made the paper. It's really something that Mrs. Steingold is stepping down from the Cub Scouts next year," Irving said.

He set a glass of tomato juice down in front of his boss with a proud grin. It was Sunday lunch, and Buster Crabbe arrived. "Didn't see you for breakfast. Did you eat all the bacon at the diner this morning?" Abe kidded.

Often, the famous swimmer who had won the 1932 Olympic gold medal for the 400-meter freestyle swimming event chose to leave the grounds to eat non-kosher food. He was currently the director of water activities and officiated the swimming races at the indoor pool. When he taught guests how to swim, they were often shocked to learn who their teacher was.

Dotty, dressed in her yellow uniform, carrying Linda on her hip, was suddenly in the doorway. He raced to her side.

"Clem came down with a stomach bug. She can't watch Linda for the rest of the day. Al is with a friend. Here, you take her. I have to set up my station." She spoke to Linda using the nickname she'd given her, "Be good, Mamashanilla."

"Wait!" he yelled after her. "Can't your parents help?"

"They are at *shul* to say *Kaddish* for my papa's cousin. I have to collect my tips for the week."

Abe frowned over the pickle he was thrust into and kissed the top of Linda's *keppie*. "Come on, Linda, we'll get you some apple juice."

"Let me come to your rescue," Buster offered, rising out of his seat and setting down his half-eaten pastry. "I'll take Linda to the pool."

"You don't mind?" Abe asked incredulously.

"She's as cute as a button. I'll teach her to make a whale spray with her hand."

"Can we ride the elevator?" Linda asked.

"Absolutely," Buster said with a smile.

From the moment Abe had introduced his children to the new lift car that went up and down, they had been fascinated by it. Arthur Winarick's hotel was one of the first in the mountains with an elevator.

"All right, I'll come get her as soon as I'm done in here." Abe placed Linda on the ground and knelt to hug her goodbye. She was a fine swimmer already. She had been taking lessons at the Concord inside the tropical indoor pool that opened in 1951.

As Buster walked away with Linda, Buddy Hackett swaggered in for breakfast, Sherry Dubois on his arm. Upon reaching their table, Buddy picked up his water glass and tapped a butter knife on the side. Clearing his throat, he told the room, "I'd like to make a toast to my beautiful fiancée for putting on the most marvelous show last night."

Abe applauded along with the rest of the room. The meal flew by.

While pouring hot coffee, Abe heard Sherry tell Buddy, "I'm off to get my hair cut at Gluck's Hillside."

Abe hurried through cleanup and tromped through the hotel, ending up at the outdoor swimming pool. The size of it was staggering—sixty feet wide by one hundred forty-four feet long. The Concord's very own staff engineer had designed it.

He saw Linda bobbing up and down in the water, accompanied by Buster. He wove around chaise lounge chairs with sunbathing guests to get to her. She looked small, swallowed up by the large pool. He bent down and reached for her arm, pulling her back to land.

"She was an angel, Abey," Buster told him.

He wrapped a towel around Linda's shoulders and scooped her into his arms.

"Did you know he won an Olympic gold medal for swimming, Daddy?"

"I sure did. He was Flash Gordon. He also played Tarzan in the movie *Tarzan the Fearless* and had his own TV program called *The Buster Crabbe Show*." All that meant very little to Linda, but one day she would be able to brag about who her impromptu babysitter was for an afternoon.

"Can we visit Marv now?" Linda asked.

"Ah, your sweet tooth has kicked in."

Marv, the owner of the Sundry Shop, greeted them wearing his signature snazzy navy-blue vest with six gold buttons. Abe almost did not see the small woman zipping up her change purse at the counter. She had a copy of the *Republican Watchman* tucked under her arm.

"My wife is on page three!" he said.

The woman did not meet his eye; instead, she took quick steps toward the exit and tripped near the entrance. Luckily, she caught her fall by leaning into the door frame. Before Abe had a chance to see if she was okay, she disappeared down the hallway.

Linda was bouncing up and down on her tippy toes. Marv made a show of bending down and reaching under the counter. He stood back up and presented her with a Tootsie Roll Pop and a licorice stick. She snatched the candy out of his hands.

"How are things in the staff dining room?"

"It's hectic these days."

Marv waved his hands around his shop. "I need to restock the shelves already. We are lucky the Concord is the place to be." He patted his pockets.

Abe would always have a tender spot in his heart for the shopkeeper. He had played a significant role in helping Hershel escape and survive the wild events of 1944.

"Can I please have a piece of bubble gum?" Linda asked.

Abe told her, "You've had enough sugar for now. How does a balloon sound?"

Wired on sugar, Linda ran right into the hallway. She received an animal-shaped balloon figure from the balloon man. Then they listened to a Broadway actor read to the audience from a playbook, but Linda got bored quickly.

Abe did a double take when Shecky Greene swept by in a full-length mink coat, followed by the multi-talented Jimmy Durante, who stopped at Linda's feet and started making silly faces at her.

Irving Cohen was charging at Bill Graham, fists swinging. "I saw you running off after both breakfast and lunch with food from my dining room for your card games. You're stealing!"

Abe rolled up his shirt sleeves, expecting to run interference. A crying Linda clung to his side. The guests in the vicinity were getting a real show.

Sherry Dubois squatted down at Linda's eye level, wiping her tears away with a tissue. "Come with me. My hair appointment has been postponed for an hour. We'll get a malt shake at the coffee shop."

Abe was relieved to get Linda away from the wild scene. When someone screamed, "Gluck's Hillside is on fire!" mania filled the air.

Chapter 9

DOTTY

Gluck's Hillside, up on a mountain and across from the Concord, with a front-row view of Kiamesha Lake, was ablaze. Flames shot out far and near. Loud sirens from emergency vehicles blared. The 80-room hotel, so exclusive that often guests made reservations two years in advance, was in dire danger of crumbling.

It was before dinnertime, and Dotty was just about to change into her white uniform when the neighborhood was in a full-fledged panic. She hustled to the scene.

Buddy Hackett was howling his fiancée's name, "Sherry! Sherry!"

Dotty bowed her head to the ground, reciting a *brucha* for Sherry and everyone else unaccounted for inside the building. She raised her head and saw Buddy being restrained, frantic to run into the fire. He had already stripped off his shoes, his watch, and his jacket.

Eva came to a halt beside Dotty and put her hand to her heart. "Did another gangster's mother burn it down while feeding the stray cats?"

Dotty appreciated her friend's presence. Everything else seemed trivial as they witnessed a life-threatening situation.

"*Oy vey*. Our wedding was so special. It's a real shame that the place is burning to the ground," said Eva.

"It was one of the most beautiful weddings I've ever attended." Dotty vividly remembered the chuppah decorated with white lilies and pink silk chiffon sitting poolside at Gluck's. It was incomprehensible that now the cabanas surrounding the pool were burning to the ground.

"Sherry, where are you?" Buddy was shrieking, still restrained.

Dotty's nerves were a mess as the fire crackled. Her mind flashed back to when the Rio Cabana, the Concord's old nightclub, burned to the ground. Her stomach sank with each passing second.

Abe came barreling over.

"Where's Linda?!" she yelled.

"Sherry Dubois is watching her."

"Sherry!" Buddy howled.

Dotty's heart was frozen. She was stuck in a bucket of cement—unable to move or speak.

Abe squeezed her hand and yelled loud enough for Buddy to hear, as well, "They're safe inside the Concord."

A very solemn Buddy shot back to the hotel.

Dotty regained movement along with her voice. Still distraught for those unaccounted for, she held onto Abe. He stared up at the sky. "Al, please help everyone evacuate from the fire without injury."

Dotty, too, prayed that Abe's deceased older brother could somehow help the situation. Moments later, they believed Al had answered their prayers when the last guests were carried out of the building by firefighters.

"What a tragedy that a showgirl left candles burning," Arthur Winarick said.

"This was all a preventable accident?" Abe gasped.

"The candle tipped over and ignited the

mattress." Standing next to Arthur was his nephew, Gordon, who held the title of executive director at the Concord and focused a lot of his time on the logistics of the kitchen.

Dotty bit her bottom lip. She was imagining how lousy the showgirl must feel. There was a pretty high chance that Gluck's would not be able to recover from the damage.

Eva, tugging at her white apron, said, "Let's get dinner over with. Round 2 of poker is at Bill Graham's bungalow right afterward."

Leon must have been listening. He blocked his wife's path. "Don't you think you ought to stay away from Irving's nemesis?"

Empathetic to Leon's concern, keeping Eva away from a good gamble was next to impossible, and they both knew it. She bit her bottom lip once again as Eva swatted her hand through the air.

"There's enough time for me to drop the children off at my parents'," Dotty told Abe. The fire was subsiding as she crossed the street.

CHAPTER 10

ABE

Abe was still at Gluck's assisting wherever he was needed when Hershel said, "We'll go over to the Rib Room & Pussy Cat Lounge for a nice cold beverage."

Leon, directly to his left, was scowling.

"You'll come with us," Abe said, ignoring his friend's discomfort. "We're celebrating that nobody perished in the fire. We'll have just one scotch before dinner preparations." For a moment, his thoughts flickered to his older brother Milt, who, as a young boy, had died in a fire because he had picked up a match and a tin of shoe polish while Ma had left them unattended on the summer porch. Abe was only a baby and escaped unharmed with Al. It was hard to believe that for a short period, Abe had two living older brothers. Shaking off the sad thought, he snapped his fingers toward the lounge.

"How High the Moon" by Les Paul and Mary Ford streamed out of the jukebox. The dusky ambiance was welcoming. All three of them saddled up to the bar—Abe in the middle—and ordered scotch.

"What a fright." Hershel threw his drink back.

Abe followed suit. A tall man wearing an unbuttoned sequined shirt, shiny shoes, a wild copper wig, and heavy makeup was zipping by.

Hershel said, "Keri April is here."

Abe peered at the female impersonator. Keri was the late-show performer at the Flagler Hotel.

"I wonder if he will sing in Yiddish, Italian, or English tonight?" It was a surprise what you would get from Kerri until it was showtime.

Leon had his head bent down reading a newspaper left behind by the previous patron. In one swift movement, he was off his bar stool and shouting at Hershel, "Authorities are pursuing finding Drucker's missing money! My wife could be in danger. I thought this saga was over a long time ago." He buried his head in his hands.

"We need Sy." Abe was wishing he had his current phone number. Sy only visited the Catskills periodically now.

Hershel bared his teeth. "You can count on me in tough times, you know."

Leon pulled dollar bills out of his wallet to settle the bill. Hershel fled without so much as a goodbye.

Abe's heart beat out of his chest. Hershel was gone before he had a chance to ask him about the house photograph.

CHAPTER 11

DOTTY

At home, Dotty threw her yellow uniform right into the washer and spritzed herself with plenty of perfume. Then she loaded the children into their mint green Chrysler Windsor and drove to South Fallsburg. She gripped the steering wheel and said *bruchas* for everyone being unharmed in the fire.

"I don't want to see another bar mitzvah slideshow or square dance again," Al complained from the back seat.

"Will there be a soup-eating contest?" Linda asked from beside him.

"You know you'll have fun no matter what you do." She kept her voice cheerful. She finished the prayer that she was in the middle of reciting and drove up the hillside toward the 10-foot-tall, blue-painted, wooden Levner's Bungalows sign. Dense forest surrounded the 34-count bungalow colony nestled near the Neversink River.

"There's a big fire!" Al yelled at Papa, who was carrying a jar of milk into his single-bedroom, white-painted summer home.

"The hotel is burning down!" Linda shouted.

"*Oy vey.*" Papa furrowed his bushy gray eyebrows.

A tabby cat darted out of the bushes, crossing Dotty's path as she explained, "It's not the Concord, and there were no fatalities. We wanted the children out of the neighborhood due to all the smoke. Clem is sick."

Papa relaxed his facial expression. "They're always welcome here, Dorothy."

She lit a Lucky Strike, relieved to have a safe place for the kids to stay. "Where's Ma?"

"The hack hadn't even stopped yet, and she was running to the card game inside the casino."

"You're barely exaggerating." Ma enjoyed playing cards just as much as Eva did. "How was *shul?*"

"I completed the *minyan* and honored my cousin." A *minyan* consists of ten Jewish men who are required for religious obligations and prayers.

The children clanked open the screen door onto the porch, which was jammed with mismatched furniture. Dotty sniffed at the air and made her way to the compact kitchen. *Aha!* She detected chicken *schmaltz.*

"Your mother has been cooking up a storm in preparation for your sister and her *kinders'* visit soon," said Papa.

Ma's out-of-this-world chocolate chip *mandelbroit* caught her eye. Dotty extended her arm and snatched one from the cookie platter resting on the green chrome table. "Delicious!"

Both Al and Linda were by her side, palms open. She dished out two more pieces. Papa could not resist sneaking one. Agreeing with her sentiment, he covered the platter with a tea towel to prevent them from devouring Ma's hard work in a single sitting.

"I'll *schmear* some *yagde* jam on rye bread. Your mother also made a lovely batch of it." Papa rested the jar of milk beside the *mandelbroit.*

She flattened the hemline of her skirt. Her sister Selma's annual one-week stay in the country was a highlight of the summer. Selma, her husband, and their two kids lived in New Jersey the rest of the year.

Dotty's mind flitted to childhood when she and her

sister shared a sleeper sofa in the living room of their small apartment. The Jerome Avenue train rumbled by their heads. They had eventually grown desensitized to it. Papa had been a wallpaper hanger, and money had been scarce.

"Can we go milk the cows together?" Linda was eyeing the jar of milk.

"Later, *Bubalah*." Papa motioned toward the checkerboard. Al and Linda scurried to the corner of the porch and began pushing black and red pieces around the marble board.

Dotty looked out at all the cows in the distance. She watched the owner, Harry Levner, tending to his cattle on his 200 acres of land. The jar of milk that Papa had carried home was the freshest you could find—a perk bestowed to her parents solely due to the fact that their summer bungalow colony was situated on a dairy farm.

The Levners added the bungalow colony years after establishing the farm. They had realized they needed the additional income it would bring.

A raspy voice belted through the loudspeaker, "The sock man is here!"

Women, swinging their handbags, beelined to the white Volkswagen van while Dotty spied an envelope addressed to her parents, Merke and Isaac, peeking from beneath a Sears, Roebuck & Co. catalog. "Who do you know in Israel?"

"A cousin originally from Bialystok. She says she's the only survivor from Europe." Papa knocked the checkers to the side before setting the plate of *yagde* jam on rye bread smack dab in the middle of the board.

Dotty removed the letter from the envelope and made herself comfortable inside a worn wicker rocking chair. The cousin's retelling of her village burning down during the war was heartbreaking. Unlike today's fire, there had been fatalities. The next paragraph about being sent to Auschwitz was painful to read.

Dotty unabashedly let the tears stream down her cheeks as she learned about her tragic family history. She stared out at the lush landscape with tremendous sadness. She remembered Papa receiving letters from his family in Poland throughout her childhood, begging for *nosh* and money. All correspondence had stopped once the Nazis took control.

She wiped tears away with the handkerchief Papa handed to her and put the letter back under the Sears, Roebuck & Co. catalog.

"Dorothy, my *gute meydl*. I'm proud that you have such a tender heart when our distant relatives are concerned."

Making a conscious shift to focus on the present rather than the past, she could not resist stealing the crusts that the children had discarded on their plates. She dipped them in the leftover *yagde* jam. Her ma's skills in the kitchen were out of this world.

The screen door announced Ma was home. She wore a sun hat with a bow over her bottle-blonde frizzy hair. "There's a cooking demonstration in the casino. Come, *kinder*, you'll see how *kreplach* are made. We'll play Bingo after."

"I'll be by for the refreshments." Papa winked and ran a comb through his thinning gray hair.

"Is it movie night?" Linda asked, leaping down the steps, landing on a patch of grass in need of cutting.

"Not tonight," Ma said. Al trotted alongside them like a trooper.

Papa perched himself on a folding chair. Dotty could tell he was already picturing Ma whipping up a batch of homemade soup dumplings.

"Murray told me there's a real possibility that Eddie Fisher and Debbie Reynolds will be the next famous couple to tie the knot after Buddy Hackett and Sherry DuBois."

"Who knew you were such a *yenta*?" she teased.

"Murray brings me daily reports. He spotted Phil Foster on Route 17 last weekend, and about 15 minutes later, he saw Jane Kean at a stoplight in town. Don Rickles is rumored to be in the area as well." Papa let out a whistle. "It's a busy time up in the mountains."

Papa's dear friend, Murray, and his wife, Leah, were part of the core group of ten to twelve families that returned to Levner's Bungalows each summer. Once her parents started staying there, they became fast friends. Murray was full of accurate gossip. She was tickled to hear it and enjoyed the lively chatter.

"The Brown's is hosting the world premiere of *Living it Up*. Jerry Lewis must also be in Sullivan County." Papa paused to take a drink of water. "It's really something how Charles and Lillian Brown took Jerry under their wing when, over the years, he stayed at their hotel with his family. Jerry's name recognition enticing guests sure is special."

"Doesn't Dean Martin star in that picture with him?"

Papa nodded.

"Well, where is he?" She thought back to seeing Jerry Lewis and Dean Martin perform on the inaugural night of the Cordillion Room's opening at the Concord. They had left her in stitches.

"Murray said they aren't speaking."

Curious about what caused the rift, she glanced at her watch—it was time to toodle-oo.

"Don't forget *The Ed Sullivan Show* is on tonight," Papa reminded her.

"How could I forget? I always wake up Monday morning with sore stomach muscles from laughing at the funny comedians he has on the show."

"And don't forget the buffet dinner and traveling Yiddish show are tomorrow evening."

"The children have been looking forward to it." She waved goodbye to Papa.

Murray cut through the bushes. "What do you think about the money hunt?"

"Huh?" she scratched her ear.

"The feds have reopened the search for Drucker's 'bootleg bounty!' They want to find it once and for all."

Her stomach lurched. She breathed in and out, counting to ten and focusing on Harry's wife, Rose, who was pinning sheets to a clothesline. A cocker spaniel was chasing a butterfly nearby. Murray was batting at a bee buzzing around his head as she sped off.

Descending the hillside, she saw Harry Levner heading into the thicket, an ax swung over his shoulder. *If the Drucker stuff is going to be in the spotlight once more, I might need my own weapon.*

Back in Kiamesha, where the fire had finished smoldering, the party line was ringing. She picked up the black rotary phone receiver, heard her mother-in-law's voice, and immediately placed the receiver right back down.

Chapter 12

ABE

Abe yawned and stretched his arms into the air. The entertainment-packed weekend was officially over. The kids were up bright and early eating Corn Flakes, and Dotty was at the Concord, hitting tennis balls before her lesson tomorrow.

"Can we go to the Catskill Game Farm?" Al pointed to the black-and-white advertisement of a girl feeding deer out of the palm of her hands on the second page of the last *Republican Watchman*.

"We certainly can another day." Abe poured himself a mug of coffee. The weekend had worn him out. Sid Caesar on the saxophone had been the highlight of all three acts. The mambo dance set had been superb, and Buddy did not disappoint.

He saw the cover story about the feds trying to locate Drucker's missing money, read every word, and then flipped to the first page. He blew on his coffee as his eyes were traveling down the page to the headline at the bottom right.

Mysterious Bones Found at Monticello Courthouse

He drank a gulp of coffee, burning the top of his mouth. The two-paragraph article explained that an electrician working at the courthouse had discovered a secret door behind a wall of boxes. Courthouse authorities gave him permission to break the locks, and the room was found to be filled with dusty file boxes. However, the electrician was shocked when he picked up what he thought contained a bowling ball and realized it was a human skull. A complete skeleton was uncovered. A full investigation of the bones was going to take place by a forensic expert.

"What are you reading, Daddy?" Linda asked.

He tousled her hair and turned to the sports section as the party line started ringing.

"Do you think you can run the dining room without me this morning?" Leon asked.

"Are you under the weather?"

"My head feels funny."

"I'll be able to manage breakfast all on my own. Take an aspirin and go back to bed. You can't miss the investment meeting later." He set the rotary receiver back into the cradle before giving Leon a chance to respond and kissed the kids' *keppies* goodbye.

The hotel was in a rather sleepy mode. Other than Irving stopping by for a glass of tomato juice with rye bread, and Sholom Secunda and Richard Tucker each having coffee with a poppy seed bagel, it really was dead.

Cleanup was no hassle at all. Marching home on a mission, the first thing he did was give himself a fresh shave. Then he browsed through his closet. With a discerning eye, he settled on a brown-and-gray tweed blazer to wear to the mysterious meeting.

Dotty stuck her head into the bathroom off the master bedroom. "Murray told me the feds have reopened the search for Drucker's money. Do you think they'll contact us?"

"We don't know much more than they do. All we can do is be honest and say the last time we saw it was upstate." He looped a belt through his slacks and buttoned up his blazer. Then he leaned in and kissed his wife on the cheek. "Don't worry. It'll do no good. We did nothing wrong. Drucker is still locked up, and we both know D.R. can't hurt us ever again."

He watched Dotty take a deep breath and pause before saying, "oh, Abe. You are so handsome. This seems special. Look at you, invited into the club."

He strutted up to get Leon. "Hello," Abe called through the door. He pushed the door open. "Hello? Leon, Eva, David—anyone home?" Not even Boychik was around.

After walking straight through the kitchen and peeking into the backyard, he threw his hands in the air. *Maybe Leon was already up at the hotel.*

Chapter 13

Earlier, Dotty had spent an hour rallying tennis balls back and forth with Rebekah, a hairstylist who worked in the salon down the road at the Raleigh Hotel. The Raleigh was previously the Ratner, still known for its legendary mambo night and now owned by Mannie and Nettie Halbert, so the name had been changed. Confident that her serve had improved enough that her instructor would notice, she imagined herself winning an entire match as she sipped her coffee. Then she was ready to turn to the newspaper. Sure enough, Drucker's dirty fortune was plastered on the cover.

The headline at the bottom right of the first page caught her attention. "An unidentified skeleton—well, who is it?!" she shouted aloud, rising from her chair.

Carrying the newspaper up to Eva's, she halted when she saw Leon on the porch. "Why aren't you at the investment meeting with Abe?" *Achoo.*

Eva swung around, holding a pair of pruning shears. "You didn't tell me about any investment meeting."

Leon was massaging Boychik's front paws. Eva positioned the pruning shears toward her husband. "You're a chicken."

Leon squirmed in his britches.

Dotty shook the newspaper in the air. "Drucker's money is back in the news, and there's a mysterious skeleton at the courthouse."

Chapter 14

ABE

Abe entered the back room. Taking stock of the powerful individuals already there, he checked every corner for Leon. *Did his headache return, and maybe he was at the doctor and got held up?*

Irving darted into the room and snapped his fingers in approval. "You certainly followed orders and came dressed sharply. Where's your co-captain?"

All Abe could do was shrug. He kept watch of the door in case Leon was just running late.

A spindly man donning a cowboy hat entered the room. "I'm here for the oil investment." He stood tall and winked. "You'll likely see a large sum of money in three months if you sign up today. I need everyone to write down their names and addresses on this paper right here."

Abe jotted down his information when it was his turn. There was a lot of talk about the investment yielding a hefty return. He could tell that everyone else in the room was similarly impressed with what they were hearing. Finally, the fee to go in on the investment was discussed.

"A thousand dollars!" gasped Abe.

The fella beside him whistled. "One grand is a lot of money."

"You aren't kidding." Abe pictured the money he had been setting aside to pay off their car loan. It had taken him months to save it.

Some of the men in the room signed on the dotted

line. Others wavered. A few said they wanted to go home and run it by their wives. Abe was in that camp. He needed Dotty's consent to spend that kind of money.

"I'd like to get Dotty's blessing first. I don't want to miss out, though," he told Irving.

"Attaboy," Irving said, playfully punching Abe's arm.

He laughed. "Let's hope it makes me a rich man."

"Ol' Oklahoma over there says it will, and he doesn't look like a liar to me." Irving winked.

The oilman, with a country twang, was shaking hands, laughing at something a man beside him said. Abe caught his response, "If anyone's still sittin' on Drucker's stash, I'll turn it into crude before the feds catch a whiff."

The photograph of the old creepy house in Rochester flashed through Abe's mind. He was itching to show it to Hershel as soon as possible. He departed the back room satisfied with his initiation into the investment club. "Hello, Boychik," he said to the cat that he saw hanging around the back entrance of the hotel.

Eva sped over and blocked his path, even before he passed by Irving's driveway. "How'd the meeting go?"

If your husband had been there, then he could have told you. Aloud, he said, "It went well. Is Leon under the weather again?"

"Leon sick? He's not had so much as a cold in years. He's a party pooper."

Bewilderment crossed Abe's face. He waved a hurried goodbye as Eva hollered about wanting to be included in the investment.

The first thing he said when he returned home was, "It's a lot of money, Dot."

"How much?"

"One thousand."

High-pitched laughter escaped her lips. "Who do you think we are, Abe? We can't just hand over that kind of money."

"What about using what we saved to pay off the car loan?"

Dotty began pacing up and down the driveway.

"Imagine what the dividends will be!" Abe picked up a pencil and twirled it in his hand. "We should be able to pay off the loan in three months when the investment is supposed to pay out and even buy a brand-new car then, too."

Dotty stood before him. "Let's take part."

"Really Dot?"

"Yes, Abe. I think it's a wise decision. If Irving is involved, we know it's a smart investment."

"Well, all right. I'll go to the bank tomorrow. Later, I'm planning to drive over to the Laurels to see Hershel."

A horn started honking in the distance, and as it got closer and the honks got louder, the car whipped into their driveway. Abe pushed Dotty to the side to prevent being run over.

CHAPTER 15

If not for the unexpected, pain-in-the-neck visitor who had landed at their doorstep earlier, she would be cheerful. Instead, Dotty gritted her teeth and prepared for a couple of tense hours. She forced a smile before trudging back inside the house to deal with her mother-in-law, who consistently overstayed her welcome.

"How come your bananas rot so quickly? There must be something wrong with this kitchen. All I ever see are rotten bananas around here. Is it too much to ask for a ripe banana?" Ida *kvetched*, standing in front of the pink refrigerator.

Dotty threw her hands up in the air. "You are welcome to go to the store and buy some fresh ones if you are inclined to do so." She glanced out the window at the Pontiac that Ida had somehow managed to drive up on her own. Her mother-in-law's driving skills were downright frightening.

Ida huffed and ate around the bruises of the banana. She no longer stayed at the Concord. Why spend the money staying at a resort when she could bunk in her granddaughter's bedroom and stay under her son's roof free of charge was her reasoning.

"Next time, we would appreciate it if you'd give us notice before visiting." Dotty was focusing on a bluebird that flew near the window.

"I called Abe to tell him, but he hung up on me. Max is away on business. Why should I sit around the apartment all alone?"

Dotty took a couple of big, deep breaths. *It's no wonder he regularly travels on business and has no plans of retiring.* She would never understand how amiable Max tolerated marriage to such a woman. He owned a garment factory—his pockets were deep, which afforded them their ocean-side apartment in Brighton Beach. Those were the reasons Ida remained interested in him.

Whenever she thought of Abe and his siblings abandoned by their mother so she could run off with a lover to Chicago, her pulse began to race. She could not imagine leaving her kids behind, with a father who was only a peddler and could not properly care for four children on his own. Fortunately, the Juvenile Aid Society had been an option created for Hebrew orphans. Abe and his siblings were placed in homes with other families who cared for them. And Ida was free to waltz in and out of their lives as she pleased.

The garments that Ida had stacked on the table were divided into a boy's and girl's pile. Dotty sighed. The children had plenty of clothes, and telling Ida not to purchase more for them was fruitless.

"I came up on a whim. Aren't I allowed to surprise my grandchildren every once in a while?" Ida buried her face in her hands. "I'm *verklempt.*"

She eyed her mother-in-law suspiciously. "Quiet your voice, please."

Ida raised her head. "My only daughter is dating a *goy*. A *shanda*!"

Ida's hearing was getting worse, and she was shouting. Dotty gritted her teeth again. *The daughter you abandoned at the age of two.*

The children burst into the kitchen. "We're bored," said Al.

"Kinder, go sit. I'll perform a film I saw for you."

Dotty shooed them all out of the kitchen, her smile showing a hint of discomfort. She would call Jean soon under the guise of friendly chitchat.

Linda and Al obeyed orders and sat on the upholstered couch in the sunken living room with wall-to-wall green carpeting, waiting for their grandmother to get into position.

"Should I make popcorn?" Dotty asked sarcastically.

Both children said "yes." *What the heck, it's better than watching Ida prance around.* Luckily, the fan above the pink stove, combined with the popping of the kernels, muffled her mother-in-law's voice.

Scooping the popcorn into bowls, she heard Linda shout out, "Bravo, you're just like a real star!"

Good grief. Dotty rolled her eyes as she carried the bowls to the children.

Ida was swaying and singing joyfully. She was also clapping for herself, pausing for a handful of popcorn. "It needs salt."

Dotty hid back in the kitchen. She opened the pink refrigerator and scanned over all the takeout containers from the hotel that were stuffed inside. The first one she inspected contained baked chicken and steamed vegetables. The second one held potato pancakes. She kept the fan above the pink stove turned on for the noise factor. Concerned that a headache was starting to burn behind her left eye, she took an aspirin.

Ida waddled into the kitchen and picked up the applesauce, removed the top, and dug her right pointer finger into the jar. "Yuck. You are supposed to eat sour cream with potato pancakes." Her face was submerged in the refrigerator.

"I like applesauce with mine. Move out of the way and I'll find the sour cream for you," Dotty commanded.

Ida remained right where she was until she had shuffled everything around inside the refrigerator. "I'm glad I didn't have another baby with Max." She licked sour cream from her fingers. "He wanted one real bad."

Dotty was happy that no other child had to have Ida as a mother.

"When I was pregnant with a baby in Chicago, I climbed up and down the stairs until I miscarried."

Even more horrified over that revelation, Dotty mumbled under her breath, "Nobody can tell me they have more of an *alte makhsheyfe* for a mother-in-law."

Ida shook the cover of the *Republican Watchman* that announced the skeleton had been found at the courthouse. "There are quite a few men I'd like to have shoved inside a secret room for eternity," she shouted.

It took all of Dotty's might not to whack Ida across the head with the newspaper. Instead, she hurled it into the garbage. She had read the story yesterday. The authorities did not even know if the skeleton was male or female.

Ida's attention focused on the Drucker cover story. Her voice rose even higher. "I bet someone is living the good life off that money."

Never having discussed the true events of the D.R. kidnapping with either her own parents or her in-laws and not about to start now, Dotty hollered to the children, "I'll be at Eva's." Then she exited the house to see if Eva wanted to call an impromptu Mah Jongg game or play a round of gin rummy. Eva may not have forgiven her for being the one chosen to run Cub Scouts next year, but anything was better than hanging around Ida. Plus, she had a plan to get

Eva back on her good side, so now was as good a time as any to put it into action.

She found Leon tying his shoe on the front porch. "There's nothing worse than a migraine. I'm glad your headache from yesterday is gone."

"Thank you." Leon kept his eyes fixed on his brown leather loafers.

Eva stepped outside with a Lucky Strike between her lips. "I hope you'll remember us, the peasants, when you are living in a castle." She glared at her husband.

Dotty let out a shaky laugh while craving her own cigarette.

"Leon says there's no way we're taking part in the investment club." Eva kicked a watering can to the side.

Dotty knew Leon was worried about his wife's gambling, and his decision to sit this investment out was probably a result of that. The tension was heavier than Ida's extra-large suitcase that she had unloaded from the Pontiac's trunk. She went ahead and blurted out, "Do you want to be my assistant den mother next year?"

Eva fluffed her hair with her fingers. "I thought you'd never ask. I accept!"

Dotty relaxed her shoulders, thrilled that Eva did not put up a stink about the assistant part. She watched for Abe. Any second, he should be coming down the mountain, returning home from serving lunch. It was his turn to entertain his mother.

CHAPTER 16

The Oklahoma oilman was handing out dollar tips to everyone. A bellhop brought him a newspaper, and he handed over cash. A chambermaid gave him directions to the pool, so he shook her hand with a pile of dollar bills in it. Abe admired the generosity.

"I don't like the look of that man."

"He's a fine businessman." Dotty had demanded he take his mother out of the house for a couple of hours, and now he had to come up with ways to entertain someone who found fault in everything.

"I wouldn't be so sure, *Abe-ala.* Those cowboy boots look cheap."

He would not heed such nonsense. Ma's judgment of character was often questionable. "Come on, we'll listen to the Latin band practice their sets for the week."

Ma thumped along beside him.

"Excuse me," said a woman as Abe walked by. She was so slight that he thought if someone so much as sneezed in her direction, she might blow away.

"Can I help you?" It took him a moment to register that he had seen this woman inside the Sundry Shop when he had taken Linda there the last time.

The woman's eyes remained on the carpeting under her feet.

"Well, what is it?" Ma snapped.

"I, uh, never mind." The woman was scurrying away and ducking into the Sundry Shop.

"She sure is mousy," said Ma.

Abe shrugged and Ma grimaced. He refused to let her attitude affect him. He thought back to the time when she had gathered her four children and shoved them into a taxicab so she could run off with a new lover. They had all been confused, ending up at their father's apartment building. After a year of living with his maternal grandparents, they were sent to foster care. His papa did his best to visit once a week. With no car, he would have to walk from one side of Philadelphia to the other.

Once his papa remarried, his stepmother stopped the visits because she was jealous of her husband's attention to his children. Abe's stomach turned remembering that time in his life. Then an image of his last foster parents popped into his mind, and he smiled. Of all the homes he had stayed in, they had been the kindest. Just last spring, they had driven to the mountains to visit him.

A young black man, whom Abe assumed was a new busboy, strolled over to the band. Watching the bandleader, Sonny set his clarinet aside to welcome the fella to sing with them as they warmed up; Abe settled into a free seat. Leaning his head back, serenaded by the sweet tones, he would not let his ma's attitude ruin the music. "He's outstanding."

"I've seen better," Ma *kvetched*.

Arthur Winarick walked over to them. "Sammy Davis Jr.'s voice is as smooth as silk."

Abe jerked to attention. "Is that Sammy Davis Jr.?"

Arthur nodded. "He's staying in the mountains for the week. Get ready to serve him all his meals."

Abe blinked rapidly. Ma sat up straight as an arrow, content now that she knew she was in the presence of a gifted singer.

"How about I drop you off to see the picture with Judy Garland and James Mason?" Abe suggested once the band took a break in their practice. "I'll pick you up right after my dinner duties end."

"Abe-*ala*, you are sending me all alone." Ma wrinkled her nose. "I've been dying to see *A Star Is Born*." She bolted into an upright position and went straight to the exit.

The man who owned the laundromat at the Concord was exiting his rental at Irving's house as they passed by. Abe waved to him.

"Nice to see you out enjoying this day. I saw Leon over at the Stevensville Hotel during breakfast. You did a swell job carrying the staff dining room all by yourself."

Abe raised an eyebrow, figuring it was a Leon lookalike that the laundryman saw. The other possibility was too unsettling.

Once Ma was piled into the passenger seat of the mint green Chrysler Windsor, he pushed thoughts of Leon aside.

"We have enough time for an egg roll beforehand." Ma was tapping her watch.

Abe simply could not resist stopping at the Canton, the establishment touted as "the most modern Chinese restaurant" when it was right across the street from the movie theater.

They plopped down into a booth with red upholstered seats and ordered egg rolls. He listened to the radio behind them while Ma took her time eating two egg rolls.

The host was reading off local stories. "Now for the Drucker update…"

Abe whipped his head toward the radio. *Did they find the money?!*

"Folks, some people never give up, and Jack Drucker is one of them—he's appealing his court judgment again."

He jerked and knocked over his water glass.

"Abe-*ala*, why so clumsy?"

He would not share what he had just heard. "Come, you don't want to miss the movie."

Abe paid the bill and held tightly onto Ma's elbow as they crossed the street. The way she ignored cars having the right of way was alarming. Her sole focus was on the distinguished brick Rialto Theater.

For the next two hours, the movie would keep her fully engaged, and he would be able to do his job.

***

When he drove back to Broadway to scoop her up, she was talking to a man in a top hat. Afraid that any second Ma might accept a ride from the fella, Abe pulled right up to the curb and jumped out.

Back in the Chrysler Windsor, Shimmy, the Pickle King's blue panel van, with its entire side painted with pickles, cut in front of Abe. It evoked an instant craving for the giant garlic sour pickles. They were a thing of beauty—crisp, flavorful, and tart.

"Slow down," Ma hissed as he made a U-turn.

"You've never tasted a pickle so good. We have to catch up to Shimmy, the Pickle King."

Ma recapped her favorite scenes from the movie as he caught up to Shimmy turning onto Old Liberty

Road. Abe was inches away from the truck's bumper when it swerved into Kazimo's bungalow colony.

Determined to be at the front of the line, he did not wait for Ma to waddle her way out of the car. Shimmy started taking orders at lightning speed. Bungalow residents were hurrying across the lawn. Abe licked his lips.

Ma huffed beside him, "Do you plan on being an old waiter forever?"

The pleasant mood turned as sour as the pickles they were about to eat.

Chapter 17

DOTTY

Abe had told her the news himself about Drucker appealing, and for that, she was appreciative. She compartmentalized the information for the kid's sake.

Al and Linda scuttled out of the car at Levner's Bungalows. Papa was swinging a wonky fishing pole in the air with an old tackle box resting near his feet. "I caught a rainbow trout in the Neversink River. Bake it with lemon; it's *geshmak*." Papa smacked his lips together.

"I guess you won't need this pickled lox," Dotty teased.

Papa tore the container out of her hands and held it tightly. Dotty's parents kept kosher, but it had not stuck with her.

"Can we go catch another one?" Al asked.

"I want to play the pinball machine," Linda pouted.

"There's time for both in the mountains, *Bubalah*. We'll play pinball before the festivities begin." Papa turned to face Al. "I promise that I'll take you fishing next time."

Dotty unzipped her purse, concerned that her parents, who were on a fixed income, had to cover the cost of playing.

"Put it away, Dorothy. They smartened up and rigged it. Coins aren't needed to play anymore."

Ma was wearing a turquoise terry cloth *schmata*, hunched over the sink, rinsing out a pair of Papa's pants.

"Grandpa ended up in a pile of something *shreklekh*."

The children pinched their noses closed. Even with the stench, Dotty would rather be at Levner's Bungalows than at home under the same roof as Ida.

"Nu," Ma said, her favorite Yiddish expression that held so many different meanings. This time she was using it as "well, what do you expect?" Ma's bottle-blonde hair was even frizzier than usual today.

"The Sullivan County Hotel Association is reporting that lodging is booked at 75 percent capacity," Papa said.

"The Concord is almost at 100 percent occupancy," Dotty told him.

After the children marched out the door with Papa, Ma balanced two cups of mint tea on saucers and placed one down in front of Dotty. "Murray told us Jackie Mason was fired last night because the owner of the Fieldstone Hotel said his act was too depressing."

"What would you do without Murray and all his *yenta-ing*?" Dotty asked.

Ma clucked her tongue, "Dorothy, that's Jewish humor for you. The owner should know that's the kind of humor people expect up here."

They sipped their tea as the power-push lawnmower rolled by.

"Murray saw Mel Brooks last weekend over at the Pines. Murray claims to have seen a hundred shows already." Ma swatted her hand through the air. "The roads will be jammed. It's impossible to double up on shows anymore with the terrible traffic."

"It's technically possible, with careful planning. If you see an early warm-up show at a hotel, you can make it to a late-night show at a bungalow colony.

People do it all the time."

"Saturday night, the Levners hired a hypnotist after they heard the Stieglitzes had lined up a magician and a ventriloquist." Ma peered down her nose. Stieglitz Bungalows was the colony right across the street.

"Charlie Rapp does the talent for both colonies. He only books the finest."

"Murray said the Yiddish group tonight includes Charlie's second cousin."

Enjoying the gossip, coincidentally, Dotty spotted Murray coming their way now.

"Hello!" he called.

"*Nu?*" said Ma when he ascended the porch steps and threw the door open.

The scent of freshly cut grass was now even stronger inside the bungalow. Murray shook the latest *Middletown Daily Record* in the air. "Hyman Barshay gave an interview about Drucker, talking about the feds being back on the hunt for his missing money. His client is cooperating with authorities this time around."

Hyman was Jack Drucker's high-priced criminal attorney, the best known one in the country.

"Shouldn't he hire a different attorney? Hyman Barshay was unsuccessful in Louis Buchalter's cries of mercy being heard," Murray was rattling on.

"Hyman got Drucker's four remaining indictments dismissed. That's a pretty impressive feat, considering Drucker never had to stand trial for anything other than Walter Sage's death," said Ma.

Dotty gawked, unaware that Ma was paying such close attention to gangsters. Her folks never even knew a gangster had kidnapped them, which led to her being fired.

"For the amount of money that he charges his clients, he better get results," Murray said.

"I thought they suspected that gangster, Drucker's Rat, had all the money?" said Ma.

"Supposedly he's been on the run since 1944, but I have my suspicions. I think someone may have offed him." Murray shook the newspaper in the air again. "It says in the second paragraph of the article here that if Drucker gets out, he will search for D.R. himself."

Ma exclaimed, "*oy vey*! He belongs in jail."

"He's a murderer; he certainly does," said Murray. "I must warn everyone inside the casino!" He clanked the screen door behind him.

The knot in Dotty's stomach had remained dormant for a decade. Now, the announcement she had not known was coming stirred it awake. Her stomach clenched, and collapsing on the floor in front of her was likely moments away. She was also shivering. The fate of D.R. was something she and Abe would take to their graves. Few people knew the truth. When they had been kidnapped in Rochester, the ordeal ended after D.R. was shot. They had heard the gunshots. The last they saw of him was when his bloody body was stuffed inside a wheelbarrow, rolling toward a creek.

Dotty was breathing steadily in and out, counting to ten in her head when the children burst onto the porch.

"We don't want to miss the buffet, or we'll all have to share the one fish that I caught." Papa made a silly face.

"Yuck," said Al and Linda in unison.

"I kicked in a quarter for each of us, so eat a lot," Papa told them.

Linda opened the screen door to go right back outside.

Striving to be in the present moment, Dotty reached for her daughter and pulled her into a hug. "Not yet, Mamashanilla."

Papa and the children settled around the checkerboard until Harry Levner's voice belted over the microphone. "The hula hoop contest is in 10 minutes in the apple orchard lawn, followed by the balloon toss."

Everyone rushed outside. Papa was trailing behind. Dotty caught up to them with plates of submarine sandwiches, wedges of watermelon, and seltzers from the buffet.

The owner got back on the microphone and made a show of handing out the two homemade trophies before announcing, "Now for the highlight of the evening, please welcome the traveling Yiddish theater group straight from the Lower East Side."

Three actors stood in a line and bellowed out their lines. The jokes got a few laughs.

"Their *schtick* is terrible," Dotty whispered.

Ma gave Dotty a look that said to make the best of it. "Well, we don't have Hershel booking acts here. See, the *kinder* love it."

Hearing the children's laughter as one of the actors pretended to trip on a banana peel helped keep her calm. With the intent to do nothing but sit back and enjoy the picture-perfect country evening, she stared at a red Japanese maple tree. *Was someone standing behind the trunk, watching them?* She moved closer to Linda.

Thoughts of D.R. crept in; she did her very best to push them away. During the final skit, she sang along with the jingle, "We hate to see you go; we hate to see you go. We hope the heck you never come back; we hate to see you go."

The silly little tune was meant to dampen melancholy feelings at the end of the summer. Dotty, Abe, and the children sang it to Ma and Papa as they exited their bungalow colony for the final time each season.

"Let's sing that song to Bubbe Ida later," she whispered in Linda's ear. *Maybe she would leave early if she heard us sing it*, she was tempted to add. She looked over her shoulder at the Japanese maple tree. Rose Levner's cocker spaniel was barking underneath it.

CHAPTER 18

ABE

Abe used Hershel's name to make it past the guardhouse and parked between a Cadillac and a Lincoln. He thought his unobstructed view of Sackett Lake really was "lake paradise at an unrivaled location," like the latest advertisement for the Laurels Hotel had boasted.

Dotty and the kids were at his in-laws' bungalow colony, and he had sent Ma back to the city. He had left her no choice by stating that her visit had come to an end and locking the door. Then he had gone to the Laurels to check out his pal's new digs. It had been such a long day that if he sat down on the bench facing the water for even a minute, he would risk falling asleep.

Hershel sprang from behind and enveloped him in a bear hug. "You made it, Abey Baby."

Abe removed his glasses to clean off a bug that flew into them. "What do you have to feed me?" he teased.

"Lobster was added to the menu this weekend. Can you believe it? A menu that isn't strictly kosher in the mountains now."

"You don't say! The guests don't mind *treif*?" Abe centered his glasses back on his face.

"The singles crowd loves it. They feel fancy eating it even if it is shellfish. Meanwhile, some country singer named Elvis Presley wants to perform on my stage. The guests in the mountains won't enjoy that kind of routine, not even on a Wednesday or Thursday."

He agreed. "Who wants to listen to country

music?" He certainly did not want to, but maybe Elvis would appeal to the man from Oklahoma. He made a note to get Hershel's opinion on the investment later.

"I already told his manager to scram."

Hershel introduced him to practically every person they passed, strutting around the sprawling grounds. The waterfront promenade was Abe's favorite part of the tour.

When Hershel saw a copy of the *Middletown Daily Record* lying on a bench, he crumpled it in his hands and threw it into the closest trash can.

"Why'd you do that?" It had been a while since Abe had read that newspaper.

Hershel snarled, "Come on, the pageant is about to begin."

"Say, what's your opinion on Drucker being paroled?"

"No depressing topics tonight, Abey. "I want to show you a good time."

He could agree to those terms. In a chaise lounge around the shallow end of the pool, he nudged his glasses farther up his nose as he counted three lifeguards sitting at their posts.

"The law requires that many be on duty at all times due to the pool's large size," Hershel explained.

"Seems like a good law to obey." He remembered it opening in 1949, the same year that Grossinger's debuted its Olympic-sized pool. Few hotels had pools of that magnitude.

The pageant girls, in bathing suits, were lining up in front of one of the lifeguard posts at the deep end. People continuously came up to Hershel and shook his hand.

A *tummler* announced, "The talent round of the pageant is beginning."

Upbeat show tunes signaled the start. The contestants stood on an area constructed to resemble a stage. Spotlights were angled at them.

A redhead with her hair in a high ponytail struck a pose, and the crowd hooted and hollered. The *tummler* tossed her a lime green hula hoop. One performance after another tried to outdo each other. It was a slender brunette named Doris from Great Neck whose series of cartwheels won the crown. She pranced around the pool, a bouquet of pink roses in both hands.

Abe paid close attention when she handed the bouquet off, freeing her arms to hug Hershel better. "Let's go for a ride on the lake," he suggested in his pal's right ear. Hershel did not budge until a photographer called for all the contestants to stand in a line, and Doris ran off.

Racing to the water's edge, Hershel yelled, "Get out of here!"

"What if he's a gangster dumping a body?" Abe fretted.

Hershel put a fist around the intruder's collar, slingshotting him through the air. "He's no gangster." Hershel cracked his knuckles.

The trespasser stood up. His hands balled into fists. In one solid motion, Hershel slugged him in the gut.

"Was he trying to go on a joyride on the lake?" The injured man was holding his stomach and skulking away.

"Probably stealing parts to sell." Hershel untied the motorboat from the dock. "Hop in." Hershel steered them through the northern section of the lake. The upscale Laurels was brightly lit in the background. Fireflies blinked around them, and the stars shone brightly.

Hershel pulled a marijuana joint out of his pocket. He sparked the end, inhaled, and passed it to Abe.

Abe puffed and passed it back. Relaxed as they bobbed through the water, finishing the joint, Abe was humming an Ella Fitzgerald song. He caught a firefly in his hand and released it. Stoned, he did not think the investment fell under the depressing category, so he asked, "say, what do you think about my joining an investment with Irving?"

"How much *gelt?*"

After Abe disclosed the amount, Hershel whistled into the night. "I'd have thrown my name in the ring if I'd been asked."

Appreciative of the reassurance that it was a worthwhile investment to take part in, another question rolled off his tongue. "What are your feelings about the skeleton in the courthouse?"

"Could be anybody, who knows?" Hershel twitched his nose and kept his gaze straight ahead while he pushed the throttle handle forward.

Not done firing off questions, Abe asked, "Where do you think Drucker's money is? Do you think the feds will find it?" He finished the joint, forgetting that he had the photograph Boychik found in his back pocket, intending to show it to Hershel.

"Beats me. The last time I saw it was in D.R.'s decrepit house in Rochester. I wanted nothing to do with that dirty fortune by the end. I don't need it; I can earn my own money."

"Let's contact Sy. He always has the answers, and if he doesn't, he gets to the bottom of it."

Hershel flared his nostrils and stepped on the gas. "One day, Abey, you'll see that I'm just as good at taking care of business."

Why was Hershel always acting like he had something to prove? He must've felt inadequate against Sy. It was not a competition.

When D.R., at gunpoint, had forced Abe into his Black Buick during the fire that burned down the Rio Cabana, Hershel had vanished. Everyone had been searching for the missing talent booker. Arthur Winarick had put out feelers everywhere. It was Sy who had solved the puzzle and rescued Hershel from Rochester.

"My hand to God, Abey. I'd tell you myself right now if I weren't sworn to secrecy."

Abe swatted at a mosquito. He was about to inquire further, but the boat jerked to the right and then to the left before stalling to a complete stop.

Hershel tried hitting the gas. "The gearshift is stuck." He rolled his sleeves up and tinkered with the engine.

Every person in sight was focused on their own fun. "We're swimming to shore." Hershel threw his shoes to the side.

Aghast, Abe stuck his hand into the water. The temperature was warm enough. He swiftly removed his glasses, shoes, wallet, and watch.

Hershel plunged in first, making a big splash. Abe was two seconds behind him. They swam to shore and climbed onto the sandy beach. Abe's nearsightedness caused him difficulty in seeing more than shadows at this dark hour, but he was still able to make out that Hershel had a piece of lake debris hanging from his head. He began laughing at the sight.

They were soaking wet and barefoot, cracking up the entire way back to the hotel when Doris, wearing her crown, came over to Hershel. She had a fellow pageant contestant by her side.

"Come on, Abey, it's time for a nightcap."

You really did "lose your morals at the Laurels." Abe hightailed it out of there.

Chapter 19

DOTTY

Dotty had woken up and spotted the pile of Abe's clothes on the ground. She had sniffed the air suspiciously but only smelled dampness. He had been out with Hershel the night before. Familiarity with Hershel's philandering ways only added to her unease. By the time Abe rolled out of bed, the washer was already on the spin cycle.

The water-soaked photograph she had discovered in his back pocket was tucked into the pocket of her maroon cotton bathrobe. *Could it really be the same house that D.R. had driven them to?*

Not ready for any Drucker news before she had her first cup of coffee, she avoided turning on the radio. She was sitting with the children, who were eating bowls of Raisin Bran, trying to dismiss the deluge of thoughts racing through her mind.

"Good morning." Abe was going straight for the coffee pot, rubbing his eyes and yawning.

Several things were on the tip of her tongue, but she did not bring any of that up with tiny ears listening. Determined to remain cheerful, she went about chattering about the day ahead. "Jennie Grossinger's bread hit the shelves and it's my turn to play lunch lady with Eva. I'm picking up a couple of loaves at the deli."

"It's about time the General Baking Company mass-produces the famous rye bread."

She wanted to slap the grin off his face. Just once it would be nice if he could help with the children's school activities. Instead, she held her own coffee mug tighter and tried to focus on the fact that this was the last summer school program that Al would be enrolled in at the one-room schoolhouse in Kiamesha Lake. Next year, he would age out and join the public school system. Relishing today was important to her.

"Don't forget, I'm working at the hotel tonight, so I won't be home for dinner," she reminded the kids.

"Since Winarick gave the Sons of Italy a midweek deal, it's all hands on deck." Abe gave each of the kids a kiss on their *keppies*.

Dotty stepped several feet away, pulling the strings of her maroon fleece bathrobe tighter, not wanting the affection of her husband.

He signaled for her to follow him into the hallway so they could speak in private. "I'll get the money out of the bank on my first break."

"All right." She nodded curtly.

"What's wrong, Dot?"

"I had a hell of a weekend between the fire and Clem being sick, and instead of coming home, you chose to stay out with Hershel."

"What kind of friend would I be if I didn't go to see Hershel's new gig? My job is demanding. I was letting off some steam at the Laurels."

"Trouble follows Hershel, especially with a gangster from the past surfacing. Look at what you brought home!"

He took the photograph out of her hands. "Boychik found it."

"What?" She took a step backward, eyes squinting.

"Mama, I need you," Linda called. That was the

end of their conversation.

She helped Linda pour a cup of apple juice and then chucked Abe's clothes into the dryer. Thankful that a tennis lesson was on the horizon, she changed into her white sporty outfit, left the kids with a fully recovered Clem, and hiked up to the Concord. The first one on the courts, she slipped a white visor onto her head to block out the blazing sun.

"Beautiful morning," called the tennis instructor. "Rebekah left a message that she's running late this morning. Let's get started without her."

Dotty squatted into position. The instructor served the ball; she returned it with force. "I can tell someone has been practicing," he hollered over the net.

They continued to rally back and forth. An image of the photograph sprang to her mind, triggering her to slam the racquet at the ball with all her might. On the next play, it was the fear surrounding the Drucker money that made her return the ball with extra strength. When she tried her backhand, she was thinking of Ida. Each powerful swing pushed her grievances aside.

Rebekah joined them; her thick brunette hair was curled backward into a bob with a blue visor on top. The rest of the lesson flew by.

On her descent home, she saw Mrs. Steingold at the edge of her property with a middle-aged gentleman.

"Dotty!" Mrs. Steingold shouted. Her dainty sun hat was tilted to the left.

She waved her racquet in the air as a hello and went to see what her former landlord wanted.

"Here's a past resident. Dotty lived with her husband in that bungalow right over there. I never heard them complain about a thing." Mrs. Steingold's eyes were twinkling.

"Hello, I'm the president of the Bungalow and Rooming Association. The Steingolds' pool is being considered for an outstanding exhibit award at the annual Better Home and Bungalow Exposition," said the gentleman in a light gray suit jacket. Suspenders with tiny cacti printed on them held up his pants. He was holding a letter-sized piece of paper with a chart on it.

"My vote is that they get the top honor." Dotty winked at Mrs. Steingold.

Mrs. Steingold touched the delicate, lacy white bow on her hat. Her eyes twinkled even more.

As she began to walk away, Mrs. Steingold said, "I almost forgot to tell you that a woman stopped by and asked if it's all right if she drops off some items for the Cub Scouts. She said a relative left a bunch of belongings behind, and she wants to clear out space. Everything is in good shape."

Dotty stopped right where the grass met the road. "That was awfully generous of her. Do you know who she is?"

"Never seen her before. The article in the *Republican Watchman* made her think of us. She seemed skittish and looked kind of, oh, what's the word?" Mrs. Steingold tapped a finger to her chin. "Mousy, that's it."

The mention of the word "mousy" drew forth the image of the clerk at the courthouse. Eager to get moving, Dotty crossed the street as the gentleman was requesting a closer inspection of the soil around the pool.

She showered, stopped at the deli, and still beat

Eva to the one-room schoolhouse.

Minutes later, Eva's white Chevrolet came peeling down the road, dirt flying into the air as she zoomed into the small lot. Dotty had to jump out of the way. Eva was holding two bags of potato chips as she sprang out of the door.

"What's the rush?" Dotty grew worried that Drucker's decision had been announced.

"There's a film crew over at the Pines. We must fix the sandwiches quickly. Lena Horne is rumored to be on her way. They are casting local people to be in it."

At a very fast pace, Dotty piled turkey and lettuce onto Jennie's bread. Eva cut the sandwich into quarters and dropped a handful of potato chips onto a plate.

After all the kids were fed, Eva tied a taupe-colored scarf around her curls and drove to South Fallsburg with a lead foot. Dotty dug into her handbag for a pack of matches. "I'm annoyed at Abe." She lit a Lucky Strike as Eva took a sharp turn at an alarming speed. "He was over at the Laurels."

"You know what they say, 'lose your morals at the Laurels.'" Eva removed her eyes from the road to glance at Dotty. "What do you expect when your husband mingles with Hershel? Be happy Abe isn't acting like a complete stick-in-the-mud like mine is currently acting."

"Pay attention!" Dotty shrieked. A car was coming their way.

Eva snapped her attention straight ahead.

"Maybe in the off-season, after the investment comes through, Abe and I can take a trip together, just the two of us."

Briefly, she considered sharing what she had

found in Abe's back pocket but decided to keep it to herself for now. "I'd sure like to set my eyes on Lena Horne. She left Hollywood for the nightclub scene, and she's blacklisted for being a Communist. Is it anything more than a rumor that she's at the Pines to shoot a movie?"

"We'll find out soon. If I get a big enough part, I'm rewarding myself with a new red car like the one I had a decade ago. Oh, how I loved it for the brief period it was mine." A faraway look crossed Eva's face.

Dotty could tell that Eva was picturing herself zipping around Sullivan County in the Ford Deluxe convertible she had bought with stolen Drucker money.

She was about to bring up the *Middletown Daily Record* article when a thud to the back tire and a strange vibration of the car scared her, as Eva cried out, "Why's the car pulling to the right?"

Eva kept trying to accelerate with no luck. "Stop driving!" Dotty implored.

"We can't miss the auditions," Eva cried, knuckles white, gripping the steering wheel.

"Pull over right now. I'm not driving a second longer in this car."

At first, Eva ignored her until it became evident that the car simply would not make it another ten yards. Eva leapt out and ran to inspect the back tires. "A nail is lodged in this one." She kicked at the ground.

"*Oy vey.*" Here they were, stuck in the middle of the road, with no help in sight, and they absolutely had to be back at the Concord to serve the Italians dinner.

CHAPTER 20

ABE

Abe slid a bowl of fruit with a scoop of cottage cheese on top in front of Morris Lapidus, the revered architect, dining directly across the table from Arthur Winarick. More often than not, Arthur now ate his meals in the coffee shop, but when his pal Morris was in town, he ate with him.

Morris poked his fork into a chunk of pineapple. "Do you think the feds will find Jack Drucker's missing fortune? It made the national news, you know."

Arthur, eating pound cake, shrugged.

Abe said, "maybe."

The architect did not linger on any subject for long. "You should take a vacation down to Miami Beach. Come visit. I designed the Fontainebleu. It's a spectacular place."

Abe was envisioning the luxurious hotel sitting on the ocean's edge in his mind. "I'd like that." After the investment turned a profit, they would be able to stay at a high-class place of their choosing, and the Fontainebleu sounded like a fantastic choice. Abe flashed a crooked grin as he pictured all the cash that he had handed over to be included in the exclusive investment.

Arthur jerked his thumb at his own chest. "I was the first person to summon him to design a new wing of contemporary guest rooms. The mountains had never seen anything like the grand spiral staircase he created."

Abe agreed. "The staircase is magnificent." He

needed to turn his attention to Irving's table. Every Tuesday, Irving's wife, Sarah, brought their three children to eat with their father inside the staff dining room. He dashed over to the Cohen family.

Leon's absence at breakfast and now lunch was making everything more difficult. He had informed Abe that he had forgotten about an eye doctor appointment and had been a no-show again. Abe looked down at his wrist, forgetting that he had left his watch at the Laurels last night.

Irving presented a piece of white paper with black print on the front. "Here's the menu for tonight, with Italian offerings created especially for the Sons of Italy. Minestrone soup will be served instead of matzo ball soup."

Abe read over the new menu: manicotti casserole, baked ziti, pasta fagioli. "It's a swell idea that Italian cuisine is replacing Jewish food."

"Good thing Dotty is available to help out. I never have to worry about her tables." Irving moved his bowl of borscht to the side.

Proud of the compliment directed toward his wife, Abe supported her decision to sign right up when Irving asked for additional waitresses during the week.

Cleanup was a one-man show. Hershel burst into the staff dining room as Abe was removing his apron. He handed Abe his watch.

"I thought you'd be tangled in the sheets with Doris," Abe teased his pal while securing his watch back onto his wrist.

"She's on a bus back to Great Neck."

Strutting out of the hotel together, the neon sign at the Rib Room & Pussy Cat Lounge lured them inside.

Well, why not? He had time on his midday break.

The head plumber and the head of maintenance, both from the Concord, had just finished up a game of pool. The head plumber saddled up to the bar and told Abe, "That sea bass steak sure was tasty last night."

"I'm glad you enjoyed it. I apologize if the service was slower than usual at lunch today."

The head of maintenance scooted over to join the conversation as the head plumber waved both of his hands in the air nonchalantly. "Seemed the same as every day. You did a fine job without Leon there." The plumber ordered a water.

"I saw Leon over at the Pines," said the head of maintenance.

"What was he doing over there?" Abe asked.

"I had to pick up a tool. I only passed him while walking into the lobby as I was leaving."

"What's that *schmuck* up to?" Hershel asked.

Abe threw back his drink; he was becoming suspicious.

"Next round is on me." Hershel slapped the plumber and maintenance man on the shoulders.

The plumber shook his head. "No. I'm on the clock." The maintenance man did the same.

Abe was giving thought to Leon calling out for two meals in the last two days while he watched the bartender pour a healthy amount of liquor into two glasses.

"You know, Abey, to me, Leon is the luckiest son of a gun alive," Hershel said.

Abe would only partake in two rounds. If Leon did not show up for dinner, he would need to be on his toes to run the show alone. They clinked glasses and imbibed.

"I've never been more in love than when I was with Eva. Nobody compares to her."

"Not even Doris and her pageant crown?" Abe attempted some humor.

Hershel shook his head and held only one finger up for the bartender to see.

Abe had found it curious that Hershel had not put up more of a fight when Eva had chosen to be with Leon. "How come you let her go so easily, then?"

Hershel hung his head. "Eva has always deserved to be with a man who doesn't have blood on his hands."

Leon's reputation was rather spotless, but Abe did not think it was fair of Hershel to compare himself to a murderer. Hershel might give off a tough-guy persona, but he was a softie on the inside. "Why would you say such a thing?"

"I wish I could tell you, Abey; I really do."

Abe opened his mouth to promise he was good at keeping secrets at the same moment that two bimmies started throwing punches. Bimmies did all the dirty work in the hotel industry. A pitcher of Ballantine Ale spilled down the bar. Hershel jumped up and grabbed the bimmies, escorting them out the door faster than the most rapid tempo in Sholom Secunda's orchestra.

CHAPTER 21

DOTTY

"Today was supposed to be my moment to shine on screen," Eva cried.

Dotty squinted into the sunshine, wondering how they were going to get out of this unfortunate situation. Suddenly, she spotted a beat-up green van in the distance.

"Ruby! Ruby!" Eva shouted, jumping up and down and flailing her arms around.

The green delivery van came to a stop beside them. "Car trouble?" Ruby the Knishman asked.

"We're stranded," Eva said, wild-eyed.

"Hop in. It'll be a tight ride, but we can all fit. I have a stop coming right up."

"Can you please take us to the Pines right away?" Eva begged.

"I can't miss Dishners Bungalow Colony, or I'll have a bunch of angry customers."

"We must get to the Pines. Can't you go there after?" Eva begged again.

"Sorry, Sweetheart."

Eva let out a deep growl. Dotty, too, hoped they could get this show on the road and settled into the front seat, scooting far to the left so Eva could have room, but Eva was in a mood and settled into the back next to the knishes. Dotty's mouth was watering over the smell of the best knishes she had ever tasted.

Ruby honked at the chicken truck, laden with freshly roasted chickens. It was also making the rounds to the bungalow colonies.

"Get your potato knishes; I want to send my wife to Florida!" shouted Ruby the Knishman as soon as he pulled to a stop at Dishners. "Hot knishes, cold soda—I have to buy my wife a bungalow," belted out of the bullhorn. A crowd clutching coins in their palms immediately gathered around the van.

"Buy two dozen, folks. I'm a poor old man. Kasha or potato?" shouted Ruby.

All the children jumped up and down, anxious for their knishes. Ruby's famous saltshaker was shaking away.

"Hold your hand out," Ruby shouted to the kids who had no dimes in their pockets. One knish cost one dime.

Dotty thought it was kind of Ruby to let them lick the salt for free. She chose to ignore the rumors that the secret spice was the ash from Ruby's cigarettes. And she purposely tried not to pay attention to Ruby's filthy hands. The knishes were so delicious that some things were worth overlooking. Ruby spent his summers in the mountains; in all other seasons, he strolled throughout Brooklyn with his bullhorn and popular knishes. Ruby was a true character and would do anything for a sale.

Eva grunted and huffed. Ruby completed his sales and climbed back into the van. He rounded a curve and then put his foot on the brake.

"Now what?" Eva spat.

Dotty saw a broken-down sedan with the hood popped open and a man with a satchel over his shoulder.

"Goose it," Eva pleaded.

"I can't leave someone stranded." Ruby descended back out of the van.

"We're late!" Eva cried out.

"You're going to need a mechanic," Ruby told the man.

Concern washed over the driver's face as he dug his badge out of his satchel. "I'm a reporter with the *New York Post*. I'm up here on assignment to cover Lena Horne and Joe Louis, both at the Pines."

Dotty was under the impression that Lena and Joe's rocky relationship had been over for a while. She raised an eyebrow.

"It'll be a tight squeeze, but climb in," said Ruby.

"I smell like a potato," Eva grumbled. She let out a yelp as a heap of pepper landed on her head. Her sneezes filled the van as she grabbed at her hair.

The reporter was chuckling as quietly as he could. "The mountains are nothing but entertaining."

"You will never be bored," Ruby said.

"I thought it a rare streak of luck to be sent to Sullivan County when the feds reopened the missing Drucker money case. I read the interview with Hyman Barshay. That was a nice scoop for a local paper."

"If they find the fortune, they should return some to me," said Eva in a clipped tone.

Dotty might vomit. Memories of when Eva helped herself to the fortune were unnerving.

Now the red and white Chow Chow Cup truck honked its horn at them. The driver, Chop Suey Louie, was notorious for being sleep-deprived all summer long. He drove his truck until the late-night shows ended at 2 a.m. so people could eat greasy Chinese food. Ruby honked back, stepped on the brakes, and unrolled his window.

Focusing on the smell of crispy noodle bowls

wafting from the Chow Chow Cup helped Dotty even out her breath instead of hyperventilating. She had been imagining the *New York Post* splashing a sensationalized story with a big picture of D.R. on the cover. Then Drucker getting out of prison, tracking them down and demanding his money even though they did not have it.

The *Post* reporter was sniffing at all the different aromas flying through the air. "I'd sure like an egg roll."

Eva was kicking her feet in frustration. The clanking sounds coming from her in the back grew louder until she saw Mendel's Taxi go by and cried, "Let me out so I can catch a ride with him."

Chop Suey Louie honked goodbye, and Ruby picked up the speed. "I'm heading to Cutler's Cottages next—the Pines is on the way."

Eva tapped the side of the van in relief. "Now we're cooking with gas." Nearing the Pines, she looked as if she might hurtle out mid-motion. Luckily, she waited until Ruby stopped to fling herself out of the door.

Dotty waved a sincerely grateful goodbye to Ruby the Knishman. He tooted the horn farewell as she raced after her friend. They sprinted by a recently built, impressive recreation building, through a regal lobby, ending up in the cabaret. The Pines was not as grand in size as the Concord, but it sat on nearly a hundred acres of land and had its own dedicated clientele.

Scanning the room, Dotty did not see Lena Horne anywhere. Her eyes became as big as saucers when they landed on Leon sitting in a makeup chair. A lady in a floral dress was dabbing rouge onto his forehead. "He must have learned of the casting call yesterday, behaving himself while Abe was with Hershel," she mumbled to herself. At the thought of Abe having to carry lunch alone, a smile flickered across her face.

"What have you gotten yourself into?" Eva asked her husband; her hands were squarely on her hips.

Dotty pursed her lips when she heard the edgy tone in her friend's voice.

Leon shouted, "I landed a part!"

"Oh, I've always known you had a secret desire to be Cary Grant." Eva batted her eyelashes.

Leon admitted, "I only have one line."

Dotty clapped. It was remarkable that he had landed a speaking part at all.

"Come, let's go see where they need extras." Eva beelined to a cluster of people holding clipboards.

An assistant of some sort sniffed at the air. "Who smells like greasy potatoes and a pepper field?"

Dotty took a big step back, wishing for some perfume. Eva, on the other hand, went right up to the assistant and asked for a part. He scrunched up his nose and studied his clipboard. Then he pointed at Dotty and said, "You fit the bill. Come with me."

Eva sneered at her, hissing, "You should be shaking in your heels, Dotty. Getting all that attention now—Drucker's freedom looking better than ever, huh? You think playing an extra will keep you under the radar? The wrong eyes are going to notice you. I'll go dig for Drucker's gold instead of wasting my time here."

Not willing to miss out on this opportunity, Dotty followed the assistant without looking back.

CHAPTER 22

ABE

The bimmies were gone, and Hershel had pulled a cigar out of his pocket. Abe intended to share the creepy house photograph and reached into his pocket.

Out of nowhere, Eva showed up, slapping her right hand on the bar and telling the bartender, "Make me something strong."

"She's working dinner; best not to make something too strong," Abe warned the bartender as "All My Love" by Patti Page played on the jukebox.

"I'm a nobody. My husband and Dotty are the stars—not me." Eva shook her chestnut-colored curls back and forth. The bartender knew she enjoyed gin and set a cocktail in front of her.

Hershel leapt down from his stool. "Eva, you are far from a nobody. You are a queen."

Abe held his breath as Hershel attempted to put his arm around Eva. She jerked away, knocking into Abe and spilling her Pink Lady on his jacket.

Abe would need to drop off his jacket and pick up a clean one before dinner. He stood up to leave; the photograph in his hands would have to wait.

"I'm also about to be a peasant." Eva recklessly lifted her glass and splashed more of her drink onto Abe's professional attire. "You'll be rich. You smartly joined the investment."

"My Foolish Heart" by Billy Eckstine filled the establishment. Abe did not approve of the puppy-dog, lovesick look in his pal's eyes.

The bartender made another Pink Lady. When Eva told him, "Keep them coming," Abe had half a mind to drag her out of there.

Instead, he reminded her, "The Italians will be a handful. Irving is counting on you."

"Abey Baby, let us have a little fun," said Hershel.

"Aren't you needed at the Laurels?" Abe asked.

Eva tilted her head back and finished her cocktail in four gulps. She set her empty glass, with red lipstick staining the brim, onto the bar. "Fun is exactly what I need. Does anybody have a shovel? I have a treasure to locate." Her words were not slurring yet, but they were close to it.

Hershel suddenly looked as if he had the wind knocked right out of him. Once he regained his composure, he said, "I'm a man of fun. I happen to have a pair of tickets to Eddie Fisher's show over at Grossinger's on Saturday night."

"You know, I've never properly seen the Laurels." Eva gyrated her hips at once, warming up to her ex.

Oy vey. Abe pushed his glasses further up his nose. Just a little while ago, they had been talking about how Hershel had stayed away from Eva because of something about blood on his hands. Now, after a couple of drinks, the exes were getting friendly again.

In a single swoop, Hershel looped his arm through Eva's, and they pranced out the door. Abe twiddled with the cigar in his hand. *There is about to be trouble.*

CHAPTER 23

DOTTY

Dotty was decked out in a gaudy burgundy dress with costume jewelry, curled hair, and lots of makeup, sitting at a 10-top in the main dining room. The director yelled, "Go!" and she introduced herself to the other people around the table, acting as if she were a real guest of the hotel, sitting down for a meal.

The director told the extras to make noise, so she picked up a butter knife and clanked it against her plate. Thirty minutes later, the director was satisfied with the scene, and Dotty was dismissed.

It was Leon's turn to shine. He cleared his throat and shouted out, "Bring me the pickled lox!"

With no other ride home, Dotty waited for Leon to be done. She saw the owner of the Pines, Mae Schweid, pinching Leon's cheek and saying, "Welcome to the family."

"She must really like you," Dotty told Leon, noticing that his cheeks had turned rosy.

Leon nearly tripped over a walnut lounge chair in the lobby and seemed to intentionally switch topics. "I'm sorry my wife is incapable of sharing the limelight."

"We've been dear friends this long. We'll survive her current jealousy. Maybe there's still time for you to throw your name into the investment hat?" Dotty cocked an eyebrow.

Leon shook his head. "It doesn't feel right for us. Not this time. There will be other opportunities." He led her to where he had parked his car.

Sparking up a match and lighting a Lucky Strike, she worried about everything surrounding Drucker and D.R. *Was Eva really digging for the fortune?*

CHAPTER 24

ABE

"What's on your face?"

Leon raised his thumb to his chin and started wiping the foundation off.

"Did the eye doctor make you wear makeup?"

Leon coughed into his hand.

"Don't hold me in suspense."

"I earned a small part in a movie being filmed over at the Pines."

Abe perked up, even if he did feel a bit jealous over Leon not including him in his acting ventures. "That's really something. I'll be sitting in the front row during the premiere." He looked toward the window, struggling to make eye contact, knowing with whom Leon's wife had left with before. "Well, how come you had to make up a fib about the eye doctor appointment?"

Leon held up his palms. "I saw the doctor right before I went to the Pines."

Abe shifted his eyes to the tables that still needed to be set. "We've got a job to do."

Leon caught the clean glass Abe tossed his way and stacked it on top of the other clean ones. "Now that you're a star, don't tell me I'm going to have to find a new co-captain," Abe teased, tossing another glass into the air. It flew further than he had anticipated. He held his breath, bracing for an imminent crash.

Leon lurched forward, impersonating an athletic outfielder. Holding the glass to his chest, he ignored Abe's previous comment and said, "I want to go to the jeweler after dinner to buy Eva something special. I know she's disappointed she didn't land a part, and she doesn't handle losing well." He faced his toes. "We've been quarreling lately."

"I'll join you." It was exactly what Abe needed to do to show his own wife how much he loved her. He would surprise her with jewelry and thank her for being so supportive. When things eased up a little, he intended to take her out on a nice date night, just the two of them.

He fidgeted with his glasses, not feeling swell about being caught in the middle of his best pals yet again.

Irving was the first to arrive for his dinner, and his energy was wild in anticipation of the Italians taking over the main dining room soon. He gobbled down a plate of Italian-style spaghetti with meatballs and charged off.

Abe kept one ear tuned into the conversation where Leon was filling the head of maintenance in on his newfound stardom. He prayed the head of maintenance would not tell Leon that he had witnessed his wife running off with Hershel. Luckily, he did not, and Abe relaxed his shoulders.

After the staff dining room shut down for the night, both co-captains trekked over to the jeweler and peered down at the glass case. Abe gestured to a diamond, pear-shaped pendant on a gold chain. "I'll take it. Can I offer you two *shekels*?" He tried to charm his way into a deal while reaching for his wallet. If it were not for the investment dividends he expected, he would have settled for something less fancy.

Leon was bent over the glass, inspecting every single necklace hanging on a gold chain that was available. It had been a decade ago when the gangster D.R. had torn Eva's special opal heart-shaped necklace from around her neck and flung it into the night. A little old lady with a chronic illness had given it to her during her last stay at the Concord. A pompous *alta cocker* had been bothering Eva, so the little old lady told her to come play poker. Ever since that evening, Eva kept a deck of cards nearby. Leon often searched for a necklace that resembled the original one because he knew how much it meant to his wife.

"I think Drucker's about to be a free man. Maybe they'll find his money before he's out on the street," said the jeweler.

Leon jolted his head up. Abe continued to count the correct number of dollar bills with a tightened chest.

The jeweler reached for the money. "I knew you had some of the Drucker fortune."

"You must be joking," Leon said, glaring.

Abe chose not to acknowledge the distasteful wisecrack. He picked up the delicate package, eager to surprise Dotty with it. Soon enough, the investment would come through, and he would replenish the cash he had spent.

"Tell your wife to wear it well," said the jeweler.

"I'm walking home without you," Abe told Leon, who had his eye on a ruby-and-pearl bracelet.

For the final time that night, Abe exited the hotel and breathed in the refreshing air. He had just tucked the diamond necklace snugly into his pocket when Hershel drove up.

"Jump in, Abey."

For a heartbeat or two, Abe looked into the back seat. *Had a game of backseat Bingo been played there?*

He shook those thoughts away.

Hershel jerked his left hand into the air, clasping a robust sandwich. "I'll throw in a corned beef straight from Kaplan's."

"You could sell leftovers like that on the black market!" Kaplan's was the most famous and most successful delicatessen in the mountains—a fixture on Broadway as soon as it opened its doors.

"The game is in Parksville. I'll have you back as soon as the last bucket is made."

Dotty still had to get through dinner. She would not have time to receive his gift yet. He eased into the passenger side of the Cadillac Eldorado and seized the untouched half of the sandwich. Hershel revved the engine. Off they sped to Parksville in style. Cruising through South Fallsburg, with the windows down and waving to pedestrians, Hershel honked at a few.

Abe sat back and bit into the sandwich. It was pretty close to one of the best things he had ever tasted.

CHAPTER 25

DOTTY

"Where is Eva?" A vein throbbed in Irving's neck.

Dotty darted her eyes around the room. Coming up with an excuse on the spot was not easy. *Where could you be, Eva?* She was envisioning her in the middle of a forest somewhere, digging at lightning speed. In 1944, the exact same scene had taken place at Hershel's farm and Kiamesha Lake.

It had been years since Dotty had dressed in her uniform on a Tuesday. Helping Irving out and filling her pockets was incentive enough. It was a bonus that she was part of the very first convention to be held at the Concord. And it came at the right time when she needed a distraction from the news.

Her busboy stood beside her as they waited for the Italians to storm through the door. No pencils or paper were permitted. She would have to memorize every order.

She hoped Eva would beat them, but time was ticking quickly. The last thing Eva had sneered rang in her ears. The joy that she should be feeling over earning a part in a real movie was ruined.

When an Italian tapped Dotty on the shoulder, she nearly jumped as high as the ceiling fan. He handed her a pile of dollar bills and winked. Well, all right, she would bring him the best cut of meat and samples of the most delicious items throughout the entire meal. Dinner was off and running. Feeding the Italians left her little time to worry about Eva; she was more concerned about the meal turning into a complete bomb.

She delivered a tray of minestrone and tortellini soup to her 10-top. The entire table stood up, outraged. "Where's the matzo ball soup? We came for the matzo balls!"

Irving, trying to appease the offended Italians, resembled a vulture being chased. "Now we know even non-kosher guests expect Jewish food in the mountains. You must give them what they want. Tomorrow, I guarantee you, the entire menu will be kosher with a surplus of Jewish delicacies," her busboy said, shaking his finger.

"They'll all go home with jars of pickled herring and brag to their friends about the heaps of kosher food served at the Concord. The convention will be a success, even though Irving made a rare error in judgment," Dotty said with confidence, stacking 10 entrées with aluminum lids on her silver tray and balancing it in the air.

Carefully watching her step, she looked to the left and let out a huge sigh. Eva was back at her station. Happy to see Irving *schmoozing* at a table situated in a prime location, she let out another sigh. She set her tray on the server stand and handed out plates of pasta with tomato sauce.

Sneaking a peek over at Eva, she thought she was unsteady on her feet, but she did not see any traces of dirt from digging. *Hmmm. Perhaps she had gone for a drink after leaving the Pines in anger?* Eva's hair was rather messy, too.

An Italian was shouting about more baked ziti. Dotty asked if anybody else needed anything before dashing to the kitchen.

Dessert was a whirlwind. The entire meal was like surviving a cyclone. "The Italians wore me out," she told her busboy as they tidied up.

Irving shouted out, "Matzo ball soup and brisket will be on the menu tomorrow!"

The staff cheered. Dotty clapped her hands together and snuck closer to Eva, who had one hand leaning against her server stand and the other resting on her forehead.

"Are you ill?" *Eva must have guzzled straight from the bottle.*

Eva bared her teeth, "I'm right as rain." She tried to stand tall but swayed to the left.

"Come, I'll walk you home." Dotty extended a steady hand.

Eva swatted her away and swayed farther to the left. "Don't you have a party with movie stars or something?"

The scathing tone caused Dotty to depart without so much as a goodbye. Desperate to spark up a cigarette and rest her feet, she refused to worry about Eva if her jealousy was going to keep rearing its ugly head.

CHAPTER 26

ABE

Hershel let out a whistle. "You'd never know this place evolved from a farmhouse."

Abe's eyes trailed along the O&W Railroad to his left. Young's Gap Hotel was a shining star of a property running parallel to it.

The basketball court was lively. Red Auerbach was coaching the Kutsher's team. With barely any free space, Hershel snapped his fingers, and several people moved to the side as if the Red Sea were parting. Abe's allegiance fell with Kutsher's for a reason he could not exactly pinpoint.

There was a ruckus under the hoop. Young's Gap's owner was throwing a fit directed at Red. "Get him out of here! Red and the refs are in it together! I'll have to call the cops!"

Red, muttering profanities, dodged to the other hoop. Abe was relieved that the police were not actually summoned. He found Hershel *schmoozing* with a couple of men from the Laurels. A sudden slap on his back caused him to pivot around toward the shadows.

"Nice to see you, kid."

Abe blinked his eyes. "Sy!"

"Hello, kid. Bet you didn't expect to see me here."

They shook hands with enthusiasm.

"I need to get ahead of some news. I came to warn Hershel about it."

A Kutsher's player stole the ball from a Young's

Gap player and began dribbling furiously. The onlookers jumped up and down, cheering as if a championship were on the line. Abe crouched down to see the ball fly through the air right before he got elbowed out of the way. Once Kutsher's successfully scored, Abe searched for Sy. Unable to find him, he searched for Hershel.

When his eyes landed on the Oklahoma oilman, he figured someone had given him the tip to travel up to Parksville for the best game in the mountains. "Howdy," he called out to him.

CHAPTER 27

DOTTY

On Wednesday morning, Dotty tuned the radio to the local news station. She drained the last of her second cup of coffee as soon as she heard, "Clue found."

The reporter announced, "A stamp with the date of August 1944 was located at the bottom of the box that contained the skull."

Bolting out of her seat, she bumped her hip into the edge of the kitchen table and winced in pain, squeezing her eyes shut. August 1944 was when D.R. had been killed. His bloody body had been left upstate, so it would not make any sense for his bones to be found in Monticello.

She opened her eyes and went straight to the coffee pot. It was turning into a three-cup type of morning. The image of the mousy clerk at the courthouse crossed her mind. Dotty had lost the receipt she was given when she had paid the fine. Abe had wanted her to go ask for another one for their records. She had driven over to the courthouse. When she asked to speak with the clerk whom she had previously spoken to, she was informed that she had taken a leave of absence two days earlier.

A strong urge to speak with Abe had her jiggling her foot while she blew on her hot coffee. She was out of luck. He was already up at the hotel preparing for breakfast. She had drifted off to sleep before he had arrived home last night, irked that he was likely with Hershel somewhere.

Now she parted the curtains to see Eva wearing a pink *schmata* and dark sunglasses, dragging her hose across the lawn. Her gait was slow, and her posture was slouched.

Dotty would call Sy right this second if she had his number. Maybe she should try to reach Hershel. The Italians would need their breakfast soon, so she compartmentalized that part of her life like she always did and changed into her yellow uniform.

Al stuck his head around the corner into her room. She yelped, "What is on your finger?"

"Boychik brought it to me."

"What do you mean?" She had not seen a chunky brass pinky ring like that since the whole ordeal in 1944. The ring was way too big for him. "Give it to me; it's corroded," she demanded.

Al handed it over. "I'm hungry."

"I fixed matzo meal pancakes with grape jelly." She balled her hand into a fist around the ring, reminding him, "We have Cub Scouts later. I'll be home to get you." She buried the ring at the bottom of her dresser drawer under her thickest wool sweater and wrapped it in the emerald-green sequined fabric.

Chapter 28

ABE

"Was Dotty drunk last night?" Leon was fiddling with a lightbulb that needed to be hung.

Abe gave him a one-sided shrug, hoping Leon would not beckon the head of maintenance, who might spill the beans about why Leon's wife had been three sheets to the wind. "Dotty was asleep by the time I got home."

"I wonder what was happening in the main dining room?"

Abe tried to make a joke out of the matter. "Sounds like they served one too many Negronis."

"You aren't kidding. I found Eva drunk on the porch. I heard a clunk and there I found her beside the rose thorns. She didn't even make it inside, where I'd been waiting to give her the bracelet."

Abe had not so much as glanced up the hill toward their house when he arrived home the previous night. He had ended up catching a ride home with a couple of fellas who worked in the stables at the Concord and spent the rest of the night tossing and turning. His mind was going a mile a minute, speculating on why Sy needed to warn Hershel.

At that moment, Irving arrived, first as usual, and they leapt into professional mode. Abe set a glass of tomato juice in front of his boss, whose chin was leaning down toward his chest. "Sometimes investments tank."

Abe's stomach sank. The Oklahoma oilman's

jolly demeanor last night gave no indication that this was the scenario they were facing.

He was glad he had kept his daydreaming about him and Dotty using some of the winnings to take a trip abroad to himself. He would sure like to visit Europe or even Asia one day. He would not tell her until the news proved to be fatal.

Full pockets were extremely important to Abe, having grown up with so little, so it was a real point of pride for him to provide for his family. Ashamed of quite possibly losing such a large sum, he served the rest of the meal with his shoulders drooping. Out of sync with everything, he spilled an entire jar of orange marmalade down his jacket and knocked into Leon, who was balancing hot tea in his hands.

The diamond pear-shaped pendant necklace was tucked away safely at home. He imagined he would need to go speak with the jeweler about a refund. Peripherally eyeing Irving Cohen stomping from the dining room, red-faced and muttering profanities, he gripped a bowl of cherries. The resemblance of the fruit he was holding to the color of his boss's cheeks seemed to foreshadow that he would hear terrible news soon.

Leon hurried to his side. "Is something wrong?"

CHAPTER 29

DOTTY

Wednesday afternoon, Dotty hurried to change out of her yellow uniform and into her Cub Scout one. "Come on, Al. It's time to leave," she hollered.

Al picked up his empty copper bucket and raced out from underneath their carport to Mrs. Steingold's property across the street.

"That mousy woman returned. All that is for the boys." Mrs. Steingold waved the gardening spade in her hand at a cluster of things—a picnic basket, a baseball glove, a fishing pole, a golf club, a train set, etc.

Al grabbed the fishing pole. "Grandpa needs it."

Her father already had a fishing pole, but she agreed with Al that he would like another one. "All right, take it."

Three of the boys were there already. They each chose something to take home.

Dotty shielded the sun out of her eyes with both hands to watch Eva guide David by the shoulder across the street. David ran to his friends and picked up the picnic basket as his freebie. Eva was en route to Bill's bungalow, behind the pool and around the gardening shed, without so much as a hello to anyone.

"Stop!" yelled Mrs. Steingold.

Eva did not slow her pace one bit.

Mrs. Steingold shook the gardening spade in the air and cursed in Yiddish, "*Makhasheyfe! Dummkopf.*" Then she squinted her eyes, yanked the whistle from around her neck, and blew into it. "We are completing the last requirement for the Lion Badge," she told the children. "We will be exploring how important it is to have respect for animals."

That is why Dotty opened a brand-new can of tuna fish and placed it on the ground for Boychik. He was part of the meeting today. She whispered in his ear, "tell me where you found that ring?" *Achoo*.

CHAPTER 30

ABE

On Thursday, Marv, the shopkeeper, was chatty while eating his plain, fluffy omelet for lunch. Abe overheard him tell Leon that he had restocked the shelf of brand-new playing cards in case he was interested in buying some for Eva.

He also heard Leon mumble. "Bill Graham has plenty of packs of cards at his poker-playing-all-hours-of-the-night bungalow."

Marv spoke again, "Bill has been dating that dancer; they've been hot and heavy for a while."

The creases in Leon's forehead smoothed out, and he raised the tray of danishes in his hand even higher.

"Bill should be pleased that a labor union is coming to the Concord soon," said Marv.

Abe was glad Irving was not around to throw his two cents into the conversation.

"There are many *yentas* that stop inside the Sundry Shop. While customers peruse the shelves, I overhear a lot." Marv pushed his empty plate aside and held up his coffee cup.

Abe refilled it, careful not to splash any liquid onto Marv's trademark navy-blue vest with six gold buttons.

"There's talk of a racetrack coming to Monticello in the next several years." Marv tested the temperature of the coffee and gave a thumbs up.

A busboy came running toward Abe. "You have

a phone call."

Leon nodded that he had the room covered, and Abe bolted out the door.

"Abe-*ala*…"

He cut Ma right off. "What's wrong? Is everyone ok?"

"Come get me."

This time, it was an unrecognizable male voice that cut her off and took over the line.

"Hello, this is Milton Kutsher. We have some trouble over here."

Abe's mouth went dry. His first conversation with such a respected man in the area was off to a lousy start.

"Please come over to my hotel right away."

His body filled with dread—the investment and now his ma.

"This is a very important and troubling matter. Your mother owes quite a bill."

"I'll be right over."

Chapter 31

DOTTY

Dotty had barely finished setting up her stations when Abe came jogging straight at her. She grew concerned seeing his pale face and his stained jacket. "Is it the children?" Her pulse quickened. Maybe it was about the stamp on the skeleton's box.

"We have to get over to Kutsher's!"

"Kutsher's? Why?"

"Ma is there, and Milton Kutsher said so."

"What in the world, Abe?" The last she knew of the situation was that he had sent Ida packing after she had insulted him. She could only imagine the scene over there. "I can't go with you. I'll leave Irving short-staffed." The uncertainty in her husband's eyes pleaded his case. She looked over her shoulder. Irving's back was to them.

"I have to take money out of the safe first, Dot. Ma owes a whole lot." He hung his head low.

"*Oy vey.*" She did not even want to know all the damage done. Her anger was festering over their hard-earned money wasted on such disgraceful behavior. With what they had handed over for the investment, their emergency fund had already taken a hit. She tore off her yellow lunch apron, took a deep breath, and approached Eva, who had arrived at the last minute. "Carry my tables for me?"

"Are you *meshuga*? I will not."

Dotty marched straight over to her busboy.

He raked his hands through his dark, curly hair.

"I, uh, I can't do that without the boss's approval."

If I'm fired, so be it. They rushed home and collected the cash. Abe doubled the speed limit to reach Kutsher's. Fumbling with her Lucky Strikes, half the pack spilled onto the floor.

Little more than half an hour after Milton Kutsher had demanded that Ida be picked up, they ran to the lobby.

"Abe-*ala,* Dotty!" Ida was shouting from the corner.

Dotty cringed and held her head high beside Abe. Milton Kutsher, dressed in a dark suit, greeted them with a curt nod.

Abe stepped forward, apologizing right away. "I'm sorry for my mother's outlandish behavior. She's no stranger to stirring up trouble."

Dotty heard Abe mumble his full name. She fidgeted with a lock of hair, aware that he was hoping Milton did not catch it. Yet, Milton heard it correctly and repeated it to him with certainty.

"Who knew he was a swindler? Nothing more than a *nebbish putz,"* Ida spat.

Inspecting the attire adorning her mother-in-law, Dotty thought the blouse was too small for her voluptuous frame.

"What kind of damage are we looking at?" Abe's glasses slid down his nose as he motioned for Dotty to remove the cash from her handbag.

Milton sighed. "The man she was accompanying stiffed the bill for three nights. It seems they took it upon themselves to disassemble the furniture and build a makeshift stage with it. The room is in absolute disrepair."

Abe straightened his glasses, blew air out of his lips, and started counting dollar bills. He paused to ask, "Who was this man, Ma?"

"I stopped to fill up the gas tank before heading out of town. An *alta cocker farshtunken* who said he was in the fur trade business invited me to spend a couple of nights with him at Kutsher's. He made himself out to be wealthy and he's no more than a peddler—only peanuts fill his pockets." Ida wrinkled her nose in disgust.

"What else did she do?" Dotty kept her eyes fixed on Milton, knowing there was more because there was always more with Ida.

Milton tensed his shoulders and angled his body away from Ida. "She pushed Pearl Williams out of the way. Then she ripped the microphone out of her hands and declared she was the star of the night."

Dotty slumped her head. Abe looked mortified as he handed the money to Milton and steered Ida by her elbow to the car.

"Go directly to Brighton Beach. No funny business along the way," he told her.

Dotty wanted Ida to reimburse them for every penny. They had just handed over almost a month's worth of pay to clean up her destruction, but she kept her mouth shut. The investment would turn a profit, and they would be okay.

As they got in their car, everything that had been pressing on her mind before, all the other madness, came back to the forefront. "Abe, do you think the skeleton at the courthouse is tied to Drucker?" She shook ash from her Lucky Strike out of the window.

"No reason to think that at all, Dot. They have absolutely no idea who it is."

He had been preoccupied at the hotel and with the investment, and had not read any newspapers recently, so she had to paraphrase the latest articles in both the *Republican Watchman* and the *Middletown Daily Record.* Abe's eyebrows raised and pulled together. "They don't know how this skeleton died yet? Or do they have any leads on where the money ended up?"

She shook her head "no" and swallowed hard. "Not yet. An autopsy was mentioned."

The brightly lit Concord was in sight, and Dotty's stomach twisted. She would have to tell him about what Boychik gave to Al later. "Drop me off at the side kitchen door." She straightened out the skirt of her uniform and fluffed her dishwater-blonde hair with her fingers. She had no choice but to slip back in and save the busboy.

"Irving probably wants your head on a platter." Abe slowed down. "But, if he's in a real bind, he'll welcome you back no matter what. The Italians are still there."

The sound increased exponentially as she stepped through the doorway into the flow of Irving Cohen's dining room. She tied her apron around her waist and scanned the room for the busboy she had promoted to waiter without permission.

Irving blocked her. His face was the color of beet horseradish. "If not for Leon going over to the Pines as the new assistant maître d' and the assumption that Eva will follow him, I'd fire you this second."

Dotty's jaw hit the floor. She whipped her head toward Eva, who was handing a guest a cup of coffee.

Irving jabbed his right thumb into the air. "You certainly won't want to lose your job now that the investment has gone bust."

Her head began to spin, and her heart was pounding as she gave her busboy a pitiful flick of the wrist to signal goodbye. She rushed down the hill toward home. Tears were streaming down her face from the day that resembled a game of dominoes—one awful thing happening after the next. She threw open the door, screaming Abe's name.

CHAPTER 32

ABE

"I'm sorry I kept you in the dark this long," said Leon. They had walked up to the Rib Room & Pussy Cat Lounge. "That's Amore" by Dean Martin serenaded them through the doorway.

"I heard you were at the Stevensville when you called out sick." Abe felt like he had been kicked in the rear.

Leon shifted on his stool. "I interviewed over there first, and then Phil and Mae Schweid offered me a job at the Pines. I chose the Pines."

Having no idea Leon had been shopping around for a new job, Abe waved the bartender over. A drink before lunch was not the norm, but nothing about the day was typical.

"You Make Me Feel So Young" by Frank Sinatra was playing on the jukebox as Abe and Leon clinked their scotch glasses together.

Hershel appeared with a straight mouth. "Abey, did you hear the latest news about an autopsy? We need to reach Sy." His voice was gravelly, and he was wringing his hands.

Abe removed his glasses and massaged his temples over the catastrophic events of the day piling up. He had not been as cognizant as he should have been about the stamp, skeleton, and courthouse news. But with Hershel standing here, asking to reach Sy, there was real trouble. And he had better start paying attention.

Leon was blowing air out of his cheeks. Ordinarily, Abe would worry that Hershel would deck Leon into next

Tuesday, but with Hershel's ruffled demeanor, he was more worried about Hershel.

"I'm going home." Leon was gone in a flash.

"I'm going over to the Wunderbar at Old Falls. If they haven't seen Sy there, I'll go over to the Dodge Inn." Hershel stuck his hands in his pockets and streaked out the door.

There was a good chance Sy was in the area since they had seen him in Parksville. Abe's breath grew rapid. *What was the news that Sy wanted to get ahead of?* Once again, he had meant to ask Hershel about the photograph, but did not get the chance.

The same moment that the first lyrics of "Too Young" by Nat King Cole belted out of the jukebox, Dotty burst through the doorway. She saw Abe, zipped to his side, and flung the top half of her body onto the bar beside him.

"We lost all the money," she cried.

Abe smacked his palm to his forehead. "Did Irving say that?"

She wiped away tears with the back of her wrist. "He just told me. Oh, Abe, you were so proud to be invited to the big table."

His head hung low as he rubbed circles into her back. "I'm sorry, Dot."

"We'll have to let Clem go. We won't be able to afford a maid anymore. I'm going to have to cancel my tennis lessons," she sobbed.

He, too, felt like sobbing, not only due to the money loss but because his pal was ditching them for the Pines. A part of him was also proud. Leon was off to a bigger position as an assistant maître d' at a well-respected resort. Abe had been part of Leon's journey to achieving that level of success. He pondered his own future as they slogged home.

"Maybe we should go dig for Drucker's fortune," Dotty suggested, ill-humored.

A little while later, when Abe was taking the trash out, he stared at their car, contemplating how he was going to pay it off on time now.

Soon Eva was outside, hollering, "The cat's out of the bag."

Abe was studying Eva's face for traces of guilt and deceit over her rendezvous with Hershel when she said, "I'm hanging my apron up at the Concord for good."

"You're one of Irving's most irreplaceable employees."

"It has been the time of my life working under him," Eva said, her smile shrinking.

Leon appeared, and Eva leapt into his arms, nuzzling against his neck. "What a smart decision that you trusted your gut and didn't allow us to participate in the Bad Investment."

"Come, I have something for you." Leon whisked Eva through their front door.

Leon was a lucky son of a gun this time. Abe was already missing working beside his pal.

CHAPTER 33

DOTTY

Abe's fingertips touched Dotty's collarbone as she stood under their carport. She was smoking a Lucky Strike and reflecting on the final dinner, consisting of hundreds of bowls of matzo ball soup she had served to the Italians. He clasped a delicate gold chain around her neck. "Oh, Abe. A diamond!"

"*Shayna!* I thought you'd love it, Dot." He leaned in and kissed her on the lips. "You have nothing to worry about when I'm out with Hershel."

Not wanting to part with the beautiful necklace, for a moment she pretended that they did not have to pawn the gift.

A car rolled into their driveway and tooted its horn. "Hello, kids!"

"Hi, Sy!" Dotty was filled with relief that it was not Ida in a new car with a new man. But still, her nerves kicked into overdrive upon seeing him arrive unexpectedly.

"I come bearing news."

Dotty's knees were weak, so she leaned on Abe.

"Jack Drucker will remain in prison. His appeal was denied, and the feds are halting their search for his money. The autopsy has been put on hold as well."

Abe grabbed her around the waist and squeezed in joy. She looked up at the sky, thanking the lucky stars above—all the D.R. business would go away again.

"We should celebrate. The Big Band Battle is over at Schenk's Paramount Hotel tonight. It's Schenk's vs. the Homowack Lodge," Sy said.

Abe tapped her shoulder with his. "Let's go have a good time."

The chunky brass pinky ring hidden in her drawer flashed through her mind. She squeezed her eyes shut, opened them, and asked, "Did they find the money?"

Sy dropped his voice, "they'll never find it."

PART II
1959

CHAPTER 34

ABE

"The real test is Friday night dinner," Leon said.

They were standing in the hallway right outside the Pines dining room. "You don't have to worry about a thing while you're in the city," Abe promised.

"I can't thank you enough for making it possible for us to attend the United Nations General Assembly. It's important to Eva that I participate in the procedures to proclaim 1959-1960 as 'World Refugee Year.'" Leon placed his checkered newsboy cap on top of his head.

"It's an honor. Now, go already." Abe wiped his glasses clean. He had only been at the Pines for a couple of months. When the former maître d' had moved down to Florida, Leon lost the "assistant" part of his title and became the man in charge. Shortly after that, Abe had made the move over to the South Fallsburg hotel and became the assistant maître d' to Leon. From night one, he was immersed in the groove of how the Pines operated. He had worried that he might miss the grandeur of the Concord, but he did not. He was very comfortable at a mid-sized resort.

For five years, he had stayed at the Concord without Leon. It felt really good to work beside his pal again. Proud of the opportunity to fill the head maître d's shoes, he threw back his shoulders and picked up a bottle of sweet kosher red wine.

Phil Schweid touched the arm of Abe's best dark brown suit. "It's a packed house tonight for Shabbat. We're glad to have you as Leon's replacement."

"I've got the dining room under control," he told the owner of the Pines with a salute.

"I have complete confidence in you. I'll leave you to it."

A busboy asked to speak with him. "The laundry didn't deliver enough clean jackets. Several of us only have stained ones, Boss."

Inspecting the dirty jackets, with burgundy on the lapels that distinguished their jackets from the ones at other hotels, he was not pleased. It was a weekend meal, but what could he do about it? The soiled ones would have to suffice.

The first guest pushed his way into the dining room and circled the tables. "My seat at lunch was terrible. Move me," demanded the man.

"Mr. Schwartz, we saved that exact spot for you per your request," he gently reminded.

"I was pressed against the curtains. There was no light. I couldn't tell what I was eating."

"We'll move you over there." He snapped at a 10-top far to the right. "How's that?"

"Don't think I'm going to tip you for this. How I'm treated in the mountains, if my mother could see that I sat in the lousiest chair."

Abe stayed upbeat and did his best to lighten the mood. He carried over a bottle of wine to an 8-top filled with bickering couples.

A guest asked, "Is Freddie Roman performing his petulant act tomorrow night?"

"Too bitter." A guest was spitting out his wine.

Every guest seemed crankier than the next. While retrieving a tie for a guest who had forgotten to show up to dinner wearing one, a sandy-blonde, hazel-eyed, big-bosomed woman sidled up to him asking for more sour cream for her baked potato. Once he brought her the desired item, she rubbed her hand down his arm. He skedaddled off in a hurry, worrying Dotty had observed the interaction. She had followed Abe to the Pines as soon as he had put in his notice at the Concord. She only worked weekends, as did Eva.

Out of the corner of his eye, he saw a waitress overwhelmed, struggling with her full tray. He scooted toward her as the top plate on the left was about to come down. Too late. *Crash!* Cold borscht and boiled potato soup splashed onto the waitress's uniform. He signaled for a busboy to bring the table more challah, pronto.

On his way to the kitchen to retrieve another bottle of wine to placate the guests for as long as possible while they waited for their new bowls of soup, a guest grabbed his hand. "I can't have any butter at all. I had my gallbladder out last April, and I can only eat bland foods. I can't eat this." She pushed her plate of roasted vegetables aside. "This is why I requested to sit with a direct path to the bathroom. Tell the chef no butter, not one drop."

He shifted on his feet, pulling his arm back to his side, losing focus as she described her dietary restrictions and ailments. Chefs hated disruptions in the kitchen routine; he used his charm. "How about a salad, Mrs. Silvers?"

"I like my vegetables warmed up." Mrs. Silvers glared at him.

"Of course, let me talk to the chef." He picked up the plate of rejected greens and went to put in her special order himself.

"Hey, you, only 12 dishes are allowed stacked on

a tray," he told a waiter, hurriedly grabbing entrées. When Abe worked in the main dining room at the Concord, he was always trying to get away with stacking 16 dishes. He knew all the tricks.

The kitchen was gruelingly hot, and the chef was in a surly mood. "Go talk to the salad man!" he screamed.

Abe chucked the vegetables into the garbage and heard a dishwasher gagging behind him, followed by laughter on the other side of the counter.

"That's what you deserve!" yelled a cook. "You drink all day, and sometimes you'll find a little vinegar instead of booze."

The bimmy held the tainted Southern Comfort bottle and tore his apron off. "I quit."

Abe had welcomed all the bimmies he could hire on a busy weekend. Down a dishwasher on top of every other catastrophe, he prayed that Phil and Mae were somehow oblivious. He burst out of the humid kitchen.

Rubbing steam from his glasses, he heard a guest say, "Dinner is a complete bomb." The baker had made delicious molasses nut cakes, but he doubted even that could do the trick and salvage the rest of the evening.

He finished his duties with terrible guilt that he had let Leon down. He was able to hear his pal's voice clearly in his ear as if he were beside him, telling him, "I trust that you'll be able to step into my shoes smoothly."

Dotty consoled him in the middle of cleaning her station. "Nothing was your fault. It was a series of mini-catastrophes all evening long."

"Let's talk one-on-one," Phil Schweid said.

"Good luck," Dotty mouthed.

He had already done a lot of praying throughout the night. Now he went ahead and added one more prayer that he was not about to be fired. In the back of his mind, he always worried that his success might disappear. He hustled even more after they had lost all that money in the Bad Investment to ensure that it never happened again.

"Tonight was a real bomb," Phil said.

"I'm sorry, Boss." He wondered if there was a remote possibility that Irving Cohen would take him back.

Chapter 35

DOTTY

While Eva and Leon were gone, Dotty was taking responsibility for all Boychik's meals. On Saturday morning, she walked up the incline and found him snoozing on a chaise lounge with his gray paws wrapped around something. *Achoo.* "What do you have this time?" Heaving a sigh of relief to see it was only a branch, she let her guard down and filled his bowl. In his prime, Boychik was a great sleuthing partner; you never knew what he was going to find and drop at your feet. The chunky brass pinky ring, the torn emerald-green fabric with sequins, and the Rochester house photograph came to mind at the same time the children shouted for her. "Have a good day," she told the cat.

***

Dotty untied her lunch apron from around her waist, straining to hear what was coming from the end of the hallway. Peeking around the corner, her eyes lit up at the tap-dancing duo.

Two boys—one no older than 13 years, the other around 10 years—practiced a routine in the corner of the room. The older one stuck his hand out, acknowledging her, all the while tapping in rhythm. She could not turn away. Once he stopped, she clapped enthusiastically, and he bowed dramatically. Then the younger one tapped a complex routine and bowed even more dramatically.

"That's some act you have. You are both very talented."

"Thank you. Would you like to try?" asked the older boy.

"I'd love to." She looked down at her feet.

He motioned toward a couple of pairs of tap shoes. The pair of women's size seven fit her perfectly. She began tapping her toes right away.

"What are your names?"

"Maurice Hines Jr."

"Gregory Hines."

"The guests are really going to enjoy your act!"

They tapped around the room, with Maurice leading. Dotty pretended she was his understudy. "Oh, this is a fun way to spend the afternoon. I must sign up for tap lessons." She changed back into her white waitressing shoes, satisfied that she had found the perfect activity to add to her weekdays. With Abe busy working and the kids at day camp, she had to fill up her time with activities that did not leave her sitting at home, staring at her coffee mug.

It took some adjusting to a smaller-sized resort, but she was settling in, happy with the tips she was bringing home. She had left the Concord of her own accord to join Abe, Eva, and Leon.

Back in dinner mode, she watched Mae Schweid inspect every item in the dining room as usual, making sure no dairy or meat touched, and monitoring the bread. When a guest squirreled "fa later" rolls into their handbags, Mae stood glaring with her hands on her hips.

Abe crept up behind Dotty as she set a plate of lemon slices down on the table. "Oh, look at you, Mr. Maître d'." She was proud to be his wife. She had been just as worried as he had been when he was summoned by the owner of the Pines the previous night, and equally as relieved when he had shared that Phil had been sympathetic about nights going awry and had even praised him for a job well done.

"Expect the guests to be energetic in anticipation of talent night. Freddie Roman and Red Buttons performing in the cabaret is a big deal," Abe said.

"That's no understatement. The mountains are very busy. Frank Sinatra and Bob Hope are at the Concord this weekend." She sure would enjoy seeing the two of them perform again. She thought back to Tony Bennett serenading them by singing "Because of You" at their goodbye party there.

Abe was beckoned, and she moved a salt and pepper shaker to the center of the table. Guests spilled into the dining room in their fancy Saturday night attire. Their personalities had transformed overnight. Now they had elevated moods for a night of exceptional entertainment.

Dotty was putting in a special request for a picky guest when she heard a ruckus and spotted Mae Schweid darting through the kitchen doors. Mae positioned herself between the chef and another kitchen worker.

"Where'd this no-good fool come from?!" the chef yelled, swinging a metal spatula in the air.

"He's straight from the employment agency in Monticello!" yelled a cook.

"A real bimmy is what he is," said the fuming chef.

Mae Schweid was trying to maintain order. Too late, the chef whacked the other guy on the head with the metal spatula. An instant lump formed. Mae started shouting, and her husband, Phil, came running.

The chef screamed, "He stuck his finger in my soup! Nobody touches my soup before the guests."

Dotty balanced her tray and hustled out of there. Catching a sandy-blonde, hazel-eyed, big-bosomed guest batting her eyelashes at Abe, she changed her route through the dining room so she did not have to witness any more of that foolishness.

Entrées were finished, dessert was served, and guests hurried off to the cabaret.

"Abey Baby! Dot!"

She went to greet Hershel.

Abe jogged over to them. "You're a man in demand. What in the world are you doing here?"

Hershel winked and slipped a cigar out of his pocket. "Everything is under control at the Laurels. I have an offer I want to share with you right away." He handed Abe the unlit cigar. "Enjoy yourself later."

Dotty tilted her head, curious about the offer. Abe accepted the cigar, glancing over his shoulder. He needed to get back to manning the room before his staff disappeared for the night. However, he looked just as curious to hear what had caused Hershel to leave the Laurels on a Saturday night to drive all the way to the Pines.

"I'll cut right to the chase." Hershel slapped Abe on the back.

Dotty leaned in.

"A Standardbred became available. He's a trotter named Prince. What do you say?"

Abe turned to Dotty for confirmation. She held unflinching eye contact with him. They had not dipped their toes too far back into gambling since the Bad Investment.

"We can't afford it. We still haven't earned back what we lost."

"You'll make it all back in no time with our horse." Hershel elbowed Abe.

"No." She shook her head.

Hershel balled his hands into fists. "I have no doubt Eva will vote 'yes' with the way she enjoys a good gamble."

"She'll have to convince Leon, though," said Abe.

One hundred percent sure Eva would jump at the chance to be co-owners of a racehorse; the more she thought about it, the more she liked the idea, but her gut was screaming that they needed to recoup their losses first.

Abe's attention was on the dining room steward calling for him. Right then, the sandy-blonde, hazel-eyed, big-bosomed guest brushed up against Hershel.

"You're needed back at the Laurels." Dotty shoved him out the door.

CHAPTER 36

ABE

Abe looked forward to Sunday the most because that was the day of the week when he would receive his "birthday notes." It was a form of kickback from the kitchen staff. Everyone contributed some of their tip money to the head maître d'. Since that was his current title while Leon was away, his pockets were already fuller than normal.

He dashed home in between breakfast and lunch to drive Al and Linda to Levner's Bungalows. Dotty had run off to tap dance as soon as her breakfast duties had ended, and Clem was watching them. Their maid was still living in the bedroom off the billiard room.

Linda and Al were eating toast at the dining room table. "Can we go to the Maurice Stokes game?" ten-year-old Al asked.

"Why is there a game for Maurice Stokes?" asked nine-year-old Linda.

"Maurice was a basketball all-star at the beginning of a potentially outstanding career until he suffered a head injury playing against Minneapolis. His friends are coming together to help him out. It was a real tragedy," Abe explained, peering down at the newspaper.

Time had flown by faster than he realized, and the game was right around the corner. He remembered the first headline he had seen about the terrible injury.

Stokes May Have Brain Fever

Today's article was about how Jack Twyman,

another basketball all-star and Maurice's former teammate, had taken legal guardianship of Maurice's extensive care. Fortuitously, Jack bumped into Milton Kutsher at Madison Square Garden and shared that Maurice was having difficulty paying his extremely costly medical bills. Milton graciously offered to hand over his resort, provided Jack agreed to get the players to the mountains. The plan was hatched to raise big funds at a charity game right there under the bright lights of MSG.

"You have a fencing lesson this evening," Abe reminded Al, ending the Maurice Stokes talk.

"I'm not allowed to use a sword yet," he pouted.

"So, you'll work on your footwork."

"Mr. Pierpont only speaks French. How do you expect me to understand everything he tells me?"

"He's an excellent teacher. You're lucky that you're taking lessons from such an accomplished man. Just watch what he shows you." He was glad he had taken the initiative and signed Al up.

"Time to go." Abe grabbed a container of hotel food.

Boychik, with a hunched posture and slow, deliberate steps, was on the grass. At 17 years old, he did not go far anymore. The children scurried to him. He purred and rubbed against their legs.

Once they made it to the bungalow colony in South Fallsburg, Howie Levner, Al's contemporary, met them in the grass. His dog, Bozo, was by his side. Linda ran right over and started petting the mutt's smooth coat.

"Hey, Al, we're going to play Stieglitz Bungalows in a game of softball. Can you play?" Howie held up an extra glove and bat. He was Rose and Harry's son.

Al looked over at Abe.

"Hit a home run and make sure the Levner boys win." Abe winked, shooing him off.

"We have to beat Dicky Stieglitz!" Howie yelled to Al.

A pair of feisty Shih Tzus tied to a tree barked at Bozo as he trotted with the kids across the street to the slightly larger colony.

"Come, we'll go call Auntie Selma and your cousins to say hello," Merke said to Linda.

Isaac took the container of hotel food into the kitchen and returned with a pastry box from Madnick's Bakery.

Abe stuck his hand right into the pastry box, grabbing a black-and-white cookie. You could not find a better one—he was sure of that as he licked every crumb. He rocked himself back and forth in the wicker rocker and breathed in the fresh, outdoorsy scent of recently mowed grass. "This is what I have to look forward to in retirement."

"Our bungalow has no luxuries like the hotel. Yet it suits us and reminds me of the *shtetls* back in Poland. When we first came to the Catskills, before Dorothy and her sister were born, we stayed in a *kuchalein.*"

He tried to envision his in-laws sharing one big house with several other families, all staying under one roof. "There must've been no privacy."

Isaac shook his head. "None at all. The bathroom was always occupied, and the kitchen was always crowded. We're very thankful for our *heimish* bungalow."

Abe whistled along with a white-throated

sparrow. He enjoyed *kibitzing* with his father-in-law. He had been happy to hand over the payment to lock down Isaac and Merke's sanctuary in the mountains for the season. They had emigrated from Europe and built their lives in the United States. Now they deserved the good life in the mountains.

Isaac swiped the newspaper off the wicker table on the summer porch and pointed to the same article Abe had read with the children earlier. "According to Murray, the game will be talent packed. The players' names being tossed around to participate in it are all-stars. Many prominent people will be in attendance."

"It's going to be the most exciting game I've ever seen." Abe was determined to get tickets. At that moment, he had something else on his mind, and he was ready to make an admission, so he stopped rocking back and forth and blurted out, "I have an appointment at an employment agency in Manhattan on Wednesday."

Isaac arched his bushy gray eyebrows.

"I'd like to see what positions are open in the mountains."

Isaac raised an arm toward the ceiling. "Our son-in-law has *chutzpah*!"

"Why should I remain in Leon's shadow any longer?"

Isaac patted Abe on the back. "I will say a *brucha* for you to land at the top."

"I appreciate it." Abe hoisted himself up. He wished he had time for a dip in the river, but lunch was approaching. The accessibility to the Neversink River was his favorite thing about Levner's Bungalows. They had no pool on their premises. He rather liked it that way, although he had heard they had plans for one.

Stieglitz Bungalows had recently laid the foundation for their cement pool.

He looked toward the Stieglitz property. Since the softball field was behind the casino, he was unable to see the children. Curious to know the outcome, he would ask Al later.

"Abe, Abe, stop!" Murray was flagging him down.

He hit the brakes. Murray stuck his face right through the rolled-down window and thrust a copy of the *Liberty Gazette* at him. "The feds are going to search Loch Sheldrake Lake for Drucker's missing money. They believe the safe is at the bottom."

It had been five years since the money hunt made the news. He drove to work, pondering how this new lead came about. Unsure of Sy's current whereabouts, contacting him was not possible. If it were, Abe would ask him right now why he had said they would never find the fortune.

"How was the United Nations General Assembly?" he asked Leon as soon as he saw his comrade.

"We had an unforgettable time. How were things in the dining room?"

He swatted his hand through the air. "It was a breeze for every meal."

"That's what I like to hear. I was afraid Phil and Mae might offer you my job if I stayed away too long."

Abe put his arm around Leon. "I'm glad you're back."

CHAPTER 37

DOTTY

It was the crack of dawn on Wednesday when Dotty woke up to see Abe off to the city. Excited for him, she was also nervous and still annoyed over the ravishing blonde who had circled around him like a cat in heat during her entire stay—she had finally checked out of the Pines Hotel the night before.

She moved the scrambled eggs across the bottom of the pan with a spatula, imagining the feds pulling an old metal safe from the deepest end of Loch Sheldrake Lake. Abe had shared what Murray had shown him in the *Liberty Gazette.*

"Can I play softball with Howie again?" Al was sorting through his baseball cards in search of his favorite Mickey Mantle card.

She removed the pan from the heat and reminded him, "You have day camp at the Heiden today."

"Last time we won 11-10, and now the other team wants a rematch."

"You can stay with Grandma and Grandpa over the weekend." She scraped the eggs out of the pan onto his plate.

Al placed the stack of baseball cards aside and stood up. He was pretending to swing a baseball bat. "Howie said he would swap his Willie Mays card for one of my Mantles."

After the children finished their breakfast, she drove them to the bottom of the hill. The smaller-sized Heiden Hotel had a popular summer camp program. It was a jump, hop, and skip away from the larger Raleigh Hotel.

She decided that a trip to the cinema was how she would fill her day. Her tips were plentiful enough to treat Ma, so she called over to her parents' bungalow.

The person who answered sounded like they had been awakened from a deep slumber. Fortunately, another person took over the phone; this one sounded alert and competent.

As she drove the mint green Chrysler Windsor onto the premises of Levner's Bungalows, Ma appeared in a sun hat, dark sunglasses, and a simple green dress.

They cruised to the Rivoli Theater on South Fallsburg's Main Street, where *Cat on a Hot Tin Roof,* starring Elizabeth Taylor and Paul Newman, was playing.

"Debbie and Elizabeth were such great friends. Eddie Fisher's a real *schmendrick.* Betraying Debbie Reynolds and ruining their marriage like he did." Ma tsked her tongue.

She shuddered over the embarrassment Debbie must have felt. All weekend long, subjected to the attention-seeking guest's focus on her husband, the same kind of embarrassment settled in her stomach. Ma did not add anything to further the conversation, so Dotty flicked her Lucky Strike out the window and let the topic die.

"Eva won't be disappointed that you didn't wait to go with her?" Ma stepped onto the curb outside the theater.

She perked back up. "I'll see the picture twice. Eva and I will make an evening of it and go to the drive-in."

Approximately two and a half hours later, they walked back into daylight. "I enjoyed it very much," Dotty said, with the vivid image of Elizabeth Taylor as Maggie the Cat in a slinky white dress front and center in her mind.

Ma agreed. "It was a fun way to spend an afternoon. Say, Dorothy, why don't you try to land another part like you did in that picture starring Lena Horne?"

In the end, Dotty's scene had been cut completely, but it was still a fun memory.

At Levner's, she tooted her horn goodbye and waited for a tractor to cross the street before taking a detour toward Loch Sheldrake Lake.

Police officers were blocking the way down to the shore. An object was being pulled from the water. She got out and crept behind a large tree trunk.

"Is it what we expected?" the police captain asked.

Dotty held her breath. The size was similar to the safe she remembered.

"It's all rusted shut. I need something to break the lock open."

Dotty leaned into the tree. The police captain handed the police sergeant some sort of tool.

A group of men surrounding the scene was preventing her from seeing. Hershel was one of them. She crept closer, praying all eyes were distracted by the metal safe.

"Dotty! What did they find?" Eva was hurrying

toward her.

"Shhhh. Don't call attention to us."

"We're taking it to the station to open," said the sergeant.

"Oh, fiddlesticks." Eva kicked a pile of stones.

CHAPTER 38

ABE

Exhilarated, Abe was gobbling down a frankfurter from a vendor on the corner, with mustard dripping down his chin. The meeting with the manager at Annie Jupiter's Employment Agency on West 50th Street had gone well.

Sporting a gray suit, he waited for the hack, trying not to set himself up for disappointment. He had applied on the spot for the head maître d' position at Kutsher's Country Club. Afraid to imagine that he would get chosen because there was already one big obstacle, he was determined to remain steady. He reminded himself that his ma's actions were not his and anyone who knew him knew he did not imitate her unstable behavior.

Back in the mountains, the hack chugged along behind the packed-to-capacity bus that drove guests to the racetrack. Abe was annoyed by the inconvenience. He needed to hightail it over to the Pines to help Leon with dinner.

Three police cars charged by. Loch Sheldrake Lake came to mind, but thoughts of his new possible job, if he were lucky, took precedence.

After what felt like an eternity, he shared the Kutsher's news with Dotty. "Oh, Abe!" she squealed and danced around the kitchen. Her face fell. "You're probably on a list that says, 'do not hire because he has a *meshuga* mother.'"

He removed his gray jacket and sank into a dining room chair.

"If not for your ma, Milton and Helen Kutsher

would have taken one look at you and known you were a *mensch*."

"It's a full-year salaried position, Dot. We don't know how many other applicants there are." Boy, would he like to land the job. He began to *shvitz*. His anxiety over Kutsher's being the one place he was in bad graces with, due to his ma's preposterous conduct, kicked in again.

"To be the first year-round maître d' would really be something, Abe. I'll start praying."

He poured himself a drink of scotch. He wanted to keep the news close to his vest until he learned the results of his application.

Dotty sat down across from him. "I went to the scene of the money search today. They pulled a safe out of the water."

He threw back his drink.

Chapter 39

DOTTY

A beam of sunlight sliced across the bar as Dotty slipped through the door at Roark's Tavern in Monticello. The small, brick establishment was dimly lit, with a few patrons drinking beer. She went ahead and ordered chicken in a basket for Eva. For herself, she simply could not resist the spareribs. Even if they were pork, they were still her guilty pleasure. She would ignore Eva's judgmental eye.

Eva arrived and slapped a horse racing program down on the bar and told the bartender, "Orange blossom cocktail."

Dotty did not understand what most of the charts and numbers meant.

"I've saved enough of my own money playing poker. I'm telling Hershel to count me in."

"Does Leon agree?"

Eva took a sip and then a bigger one. "He'll reap the benefits. I'll buy him a kitten or two."

With full stomachs, they walked the short distance to Broadway to watch the Sullivan County Volunteer Firefighters Association's annual parade. It was rumored that thousands of people were expected, on top of the hundreds of firemen in the actual parade, and scores of musicians marching alongside them.

A horn was blown, and a long line of firemen marched from the northern end of Broadway. "Is that Nelson Rockefeller?!" shouted a man.

Dotty ran her eyes over the length of Broadway.

She did not see the governor. There was a float farther behind the first line of firemen. Maybe he was on that.

Eva said, "I heard Nelson Rockefeller is signed up to be the principal speaker at the Women's Club meeting at the Concord."

The Monticello Women's Club was hosting the annual convention of the New York State Federation of Women's Clubs that year.

"How exciting! I guess we should've joined the Women's Club." There really was no good reason that they had not already signed up, other than the various activities in which they already participated.

The firemen were within yards of them now, marching by as wild cheers ricocheted off the architecturally significant buildings that lined Broadway. A lady wearing a red and blue polka dot T-shirt, sandwiched between two percussionists, threw candy into the air. Dotty caught a couple of pieces for the children.

A row of police officers came into view. "Did you open the safe yet? Is Drucker's fortune inside?" Eva shouted.

The marching band was behind them, making any response she might have received impossible to hear.

***

Upon returning home, Al threw the door open. "Auntie Jean is here with Barry and a friend."

"A friend? Where's Uncle Mort?"

"Her name is Barb. I don't know where he is."

Unable to resist gently tugging his dark curls and pinching his chubby cheeks, Dotty lit up at the sight of one-year-old Barry. She told him, "You are your mama's twin," tilting her head toward Jean.

"Dotty, I'd like to introduce you to Barb." Jean carried a rectangular casserole dish in her hands and stepped closer to a woman with short, dark hair.

"Where's Mort?" Dotty asked.

Jean pursed her lips. "He's gone."

Dotty tugged on Barry's curls again.

"Gone for good," Jean added.

Dotty gasped. "Why?"

"He was a *shmendrik*. Barry and I are better off without him."

Dotty narrowed her eyes, inspecting Barb more closely.

"Hello," Barb said, her voice warm, holding out her hand for Dotty to shake.

"Barb lives with us now," Jean said simply.

Dotty shook Barb's hand. As long as Jean was happy, who was she to judge? When Jean had dated the *goy* so many years ago, she had ignored the negative comments, so Dotty knew her sister-in-law could handle herself however she saw fit.

Jean opened the pink oven doors inside the kitchen and slid the casserole dish to the center of it. "I made stuffed cabbage following our bubbe's recipe. It's already baked for hours. All it needs is a little reheating. We'll surprise my brother with it."

Dotty could not wait to sink her teeth into the cabbage leaves, smothered in sweet tomato sauce and wrapped around ground beef, rice, onions, and raisins. She thought his sister and Barb's arrival would be a surprise enough.

Once Jean removed the casserole dish from the pink oven, Dotty stuck her head out the side door and called for Al, who was playing baseball with a group of neighborhood boys. Mrs. Steingold was tending to a shrub of blue hydrangeas across the street and raised her cane, ushering Dotty to come closer.

She hollered, "I'll be right back," before crossing the street.

After four years of running the Cub Scouts with Eva, Dotty had resigned, and her position was handed to another mom. Eva, too, had resigned once Al and David had moved on to Boy Scouts.

Mrs. Steingold was wearing a wiglet and thick prescription sunglasses. She cleared her throat. "That same woman, the mousy-looking one who donated that stuff all those years ago to the Cub Scouts, is back."

Dotty wondered if Mrs. Steingold's memory was starting to fail. She searched her own memory, and the woman from the courthouse raced through her mind.

"I'm hungry," Al said. He had dirt covering his shirt from sliding into home base.

"Come, let's go eat," she forgot about the mousy woman as the smell of stuffed cabbage with raisins had her mind only thinking of eating.

"*Es gezinteheit!*" Jean set the meal on the table.

"*Es gezinteheit!*" Linda repeated. She was eyeing the dinner with a sparkle in her eyes.

Dotty could hear her own mother's voice telling them in Yiddish, "bon appétit," so many times as a child. She cut into her stuffed cabbage. "This is *geshmak*. Tastes like a five-star meal."

"Norman is missing out," Jean said, her mouth full.

"Where is he? How come he didn't catch a ride with you?" Dotty asked.

Jean finished chewing. "He got a new position as an administrator at his school. He wants to become a principal one day."

"Principal," Dotty clucked her tongue, confident that Abe's brother would accomplish whatever he set out to achieve.

"He met Rita when they both attended Columbia. She grew up in Greenpoint and works on grants for schools. They've gone out to Fire Island together," added Jean.

Dotty clucked her tongue once more as a pair of headlights shone through the window. "Norman invited Al into the city to visit the Museum of Natural History." She would be sure to grill Al for information on Rita after that trip.

"It's Uncle Abe, right on time." Jean clapped. Barry began clapping next.

"What a fan club I have, and I haven't handed over the good stuff yet." Abe presented a carton of pickled lox.

"Daddy, Auntie Jean fixed dinner, so we don't need hotel food tonight."

"Don't you know there can never be enough food in the mountains, dear Linda?" Jean pulled the entire carton of pickled lox to her place setting.

Abe held onto a container of apple fritters and quizzically gazed at Barb. Not yet aware that Mort had been replaced by a woman, Dotty needed to get him up to speed.

His entire face radiated as he laid eyes on Jean's stuffed cabbage. "How's Papa?"

"We're meeting at the park tomorrow. I know he's planning on observing the High Holidays with you in the mountains." Jean was already reaching for seconds.

As they ate the apple fritters for dessert, the radio played in the background. Dotty hummed along to an Ella Fitzgerald song. The show tunes stopped and, sharply, she whipped her head in the direction of the radio upon hearing the host announce, "the safe pulled from Loch Sheldrake Lake is only filled with fishing lures."

Abe caught her eye and smiled. The host was not done divulging. "The feds are coming clean about a scheme they planned in 1954. For five years, they watched the people on the list. Stay tuned for more updates."

Dotty ran a cloth under the faucet and dabbed it on her forehead.

CHAPTER 40

ABE

On Sunday afternoon, Abe sniffed around the Jewish Community Center. "Where's the food?"

"We're here to talk business, not fill our stomachs," reprimanded Dotty.

"We can do both," he rationalized, sniffing the air like a bloodhound, hoping to find stuffed cabbage that tasted like the one Jean had made for them on her last visit. He would have to call his sister later to encourage her to travel back up soon. It was both eye-opening and a pleasure to have met Barb.

"Come, Eva saved us seats." Dotty pulled him toward a row of aluminum chairs at the same time he saw Hershel and Rebekah. Dotty's tennis partner and the hairstylist down at the Raleigh Hotel had been Hershel's steady flame for a little more than a year now.

"Go sit. I'll join you in a minute. I need to speak to Hershel." Rebekah went to sit with Dotty. "Do you know any information about the feds and a scheme in 1954?"

Hershel, with a wide stance, wrung his hands. "It's a shock to me as well, Abey." He pulled his wallet out of his pocket and emptied the money inside. "My contribution." He handed the pile to Abe.

"You aren't staying for the meeting?"

"I need to take care of some business at the track. I laid out all the money for Prince until you fools come to your senses."

Abe wrinkled his forehead. Dotty was waving him over.

"Rebekah is catching a ride home." Hershel fled.

"What's that *putz* up to?" Leon whispered in his ear, sitting to his left. "I know he's been trying to convince everyone to buy a horse with him. I don't think that's wise."

Abe adjusted his glasses. "What did I get myself into?"

"Eva's been proactive with the aspiration of forming a congregation for weeks. You've joined the committee by showing up." Leon gave him a toothy grin.

"I have? Well, all right. A temple in Monticello sounds like a swell idea."

"Maybe you'll go to services?"

Abe considered the idea. He had become lax in his religion as an adult. Ordinarily, he shared everything about work with Leon, so it was strange not to be able to talk about the potential Kutsher's job with him. He brought up a neutral subject. "Do you think it'll be a rematch between the Yankees and the Milwaukee Braves during the World Series again?"

"Mickey Mantle sure is having a lackluster season compared to last year."

"It's looking like it might be his worst overall season." Abe started humming "Take Me Out to the Ball Game" until Dotty shushed him because Rabbi Davidovich stood behind a podium.

"The formation of a space for Reform Judaism inside the community is an honorable quest. I thank you all for your positive responses and support in making my dream come true," said the rabbi.

Next, Eva stood behind the podium and talked

about raising funds to build a permanent temple. Abe pulled out his wallet, adding a sizable donation to the collection envelope, along with what Hershel had trusted him to donate. Now they were all officially founding members.

The meeting adjourned, and a tray of black-and-white cookies was set out along with a pot of coffee. Abe was the first one in line. He added a sugar cube to his coffee as he watched the rabbi approach Eva. She had been scurrying around the room, enthused about the temple's future and her leadership role in the endeavor. Rebekah stood beside the rabbi.

Abe overheard the rabbi clearing his throat. "Rebekah would like to join the fundraising committee. She has an excellent idea to share with you."

Eva's lips formed a defiant curve. Abe lost focus on the conversation. He began to fear that a better candidate, without a combative mother, could land the maître d' job at Kutsher's. He took the last bite of the chocolate portion of his cookie.

Eva swooped over and dropped her voice to a whisper. "I paid for my share of Prince. Come on, Abey, join us."

Perhaps if I land the big job, and does your husband know?

***

While Abe was reviewing the seating chart with diagrams of each table, Phil Shweid waved hello as Mae caught up to him, sharing a complaint about the bread. Abe was tuned into their conversation only because of his proximity to the couple.

Phil said, "I hear the Kutshers have chosen

their new maître d'."

Abe's heart sank to his toes. He had not heard any news. *This is a bad sign.* The seating chart fluttered to the ground.

Chapter 41

"I have to stop by the temple site. Tag along with me," Eva said on Monday.

Glad to have something to divert her attention, Dotty settled into the passenger seat. She had been listening to the same radio station all morning long with no insight. Now she wanted Eva's input. "I've been racking my brain for ideas about what the feds were investigating in 1954."

"I sure would like to know myself. They should tell us already."

Dotty wanted to explore the topic more, but Eva was distracted by other thoughts. "The Monticello Classic is around the corner. The best pony will be crowned then! Come on, you must throw your hat in. I know you're storing your tips away."

A police car went by; they both sat taller, wishing for an update from the officer inside.

Arriving at the corner lot of land where Temple Sholom would be built, Eva said, "Rabbi Davidovich and I reviewed the plans last night."

"You really have become religious lately."

"It keeps me busy, and I enjoy helping with the temple. It'll be nice to have an actual building one day and no longer have to meet at the JCC or the Crawford Public Library."

"Are you aware that the Elks Club's dinner is scheduled for the same night as the temple dinner at the Concord?"

"Yes. Leon pays his dues every year and we try to go to the fundraising dinners, but that's about it. Abe isn't any more active in the Elks than that, is he?"

Dotty shook her head and said, "Won't it be something to be guests back at the Concord for an evening? How come you didn't push for the dinner to be held at the Pines?"

"The rabbi wanted the Concord, and I didn't contest. It'll be like old times having it there." Eva shrugged and gestured at a patch of dirt. "I want the temple to be in action lickety-split. The gardens will go over there. Come fall, I'll recruit a team to help me plant a bed of tulips to rival the Concord."

"Winarick will add more gardens."

"You aren't kidding." Eva led them back to her car.

Dotty raised an eyebrow. "Will you let Rebekah join the gardening committee?"

Eva slid into the passenger seat and slammed the car door shut so forcefully that her skirt got caught in the door. "I didn't entertain her fundraising idea for a single second. How silly, a fashion show with avant-garde hairstyles." She yanked her skirt free and stepped on the gas.

Dotty liked the idea and was picturing a runway set up on the lawn of the temple when Eva said, "How about a game of pool? Winner gets a dollar! I need a distraction before it's time to meet Prince over at the track."

"All right, I'll take the challenge." She had some free time before her tap dancing lesson later.

***

"Come On-A My House" by Rosemary Clooney was

bellowing out of the jukebox, and a cloud of smoke hung heavy inside Kiamesha Lanes.

Eva chalked the tip of her pool cue. "Why did Hershel miss the meeting at the temple last night?" she asked before leaning over and aiming at the white cue ball for the opening break.

"Beats me." Dotty chalked up her pool cue.

Eva pressed her lips together. She pocketed the purple number four ball and the orange number five ball. "I made a large bet on the Classic. It better pay out."

Dotty sincerely hoped it did not turn out like the Bad Investment. She aimed her cue and pocketed the striped, yellow number nine ball.

Eva was strategizing her next move as the front door burst open and in sashayed a character wearing a lacy white dress, a headband with a green feather sticking out of poofy hair, caked-on makeup, and big sunglasses. "It's Keri April." Eva waved her cue in the direction of the female impersonator.

At the farthest lane to the left, the bandleader from the Flagler Hotel hit a spare. Keri pranced by him, clapping. In one swift motion, the bandleader had his hand around Keri's neck.

Fearful that real injury would be inflicted, Dotty held her breath, recalling the time she had seen Keri perform at the Flagler Hotel. He had been a fabulous entertainer. Relieved to see him zip over to the bar unharmed, Dotty's breathing returned to normal, and she focused on the game of pool.

Her memories of a classmate she had known by the name of George Jorgensen Jr. were triggered. After returning from the U.S. Army, George became

Christine and an overnight celebrity. Dotty still had the copy of the *New York Daily News* front page story announcing the transition. She also still had her yearbook, where their pictures were on the same page.

"Go, it's your turn," Eva nudged her.

From the looks of it, Dotty had a feeling that both the bandleader and Keri April were enjoying the tension. Following every peanut that Keri ate, he would rub his fingers together to get rid of the crumbs in a way that infuriated the bandleader, bothering his sense of machismo. In a flash, the bandleader chucked an entire bowl of pretzels at his adversary. Keri gave it back just as good, hurling a handful of peanuts and a string of insults. Dotty aimed at the striped red number 11 ball and missed.

Eva pocketed the last ball that remained on the table, the eight ball. Dotty reached inside her handbag for a dollar bill. Eva zipped her winnings into her change purse as Keri jumped onto a table singing "Honeysuckle Rose." It was too irresistible an act to bail on. Dotty hummed along and swayed to the tune until she overheard a gentleman talking to his pal.

"I hear an old mystery is being dredged up. Remember that skeleton found at the courthouse half a decade ago?" He steepled his fingers. "Mm-hmm, that's right; the district attorney is back on the case."

Pretzel pieces crunched beneath Dotty's feet as she hightailed it across the room and leaned across the bar.

CHAPTER 42

Not sleeping well the night before, Abe had dragged himself through breakfast and now here he was doing the same thing at lunchtime. His gut was telling him his ma might very well ruin the whole Kutsher's job for him.

A guest complained about a burnt onion roll and, completely out of character, he shouted, "You're lucky to eat at all! I grew up hungry all the time."

Leon tapped him on the shoulder. "Is something upsetting you today? I noticed you've been short with quite a few guests."

"I'm feeling a bit under the weather." He knew it was true that his patience and charm were not up to par. However, lunch was neither a breeze nor a bomb. It fell into the good category.

"Go recharge before dinner," Leon told him.

Abe bid farewell and drove home in a miserable mood. He made a spontaneous decision to take a dip in the Neversink River.

Murray came flying at him. "Abe, look! See right there, scootch a little closer. Right there, by that big rock—it's the safe that the feds are searching for—oh, I must call in the tip right now!"

Murray was leaping through the field as Abe eased into the water to get a closer look. He could tell right away that it was not Drucker's metal safe. The one in the river was a completely different shape.

He toweled off and went home. It was pure

coincidence that the rotary phone was ringing as he stepped inside. He considered ignoring it so that he could crawl into bed more quickly, but he went ahead and answered; it might be Hershel. He had tried to reach his pal earlier in the morning but had no luck.

"Who is it?" a female voice asked into the party line. The Annie Jupiter's Employment Agency was on the other end.

"It's for me. You can hang up now." Abe listened to the female voice breathing. He hoped the person from the employment agency did not mind the wait. Finally, he felt it was only the two of them and spoke again. "Have the Kutshers made up their minds?" He was on pins and needles, gripping the rotary receiver.

CHAPTER 43

DOTTY

Keri April bowed and leapt off the table. The Latin bandleader from the Flagler Hotel had stormed out of Kiamesha Lanes after the first verse.

Dotty's eyes were trying to follow the bowling ball rolling down the lane in front of her, but she was seeing two of everything. Every single pin toppled over. She applauded along with the rest of the crowd. The liquor, doing its job, made her momentarily forget all about the skeleton news. A conversation behind her caught her attention.

A man untying a pair of red-and-black bowling shoes said, "Sam applied for the maître d' position over at Kutsher's."

Her mind clouded. She searched her memory for a Sam who could be competing with her husband. Last night Abe had come home blue. They always watched the latest episode of *The Ford Show* on the television set together, but even the fun variety program had not boosted his spirits. He had been convinced that the Kutshers had decided against hiring him. And, truthfully, she was sure Ida had messed everything up for him.

"A penny for your thoughts." Eva pinched her on the arm.

"Who is Sam?" Dotty asked more loudly than if she had been sober.

"Why, Sam's the finest fella around," said the man now standing in his socks, his bowling shoes in his left hand.

Dotty scowled at him. "He's not the finest fella. My husband is the finest fella."

Eva stepped in front of her. "Don't you have a tap dancing lesson to get to? Come, someone in the ladies' room just told me there's a litter of kittens across the street. I'm taking one home to Leon. It'll soften the blow when I admit to him that we are officially co-owners of a racehorse."

Chapter 44

ABE

The person from the employment agency kept hope alive, relaying the message that Milton Kutsher wanted to speak with him in person before making a final decision. Abe stood inside the bustling lobby, observing the guests rushing from one activity to the next. He straightened his posture and waited for the owner.

"Abe, thank you for coming over." Milton extended his hand for a firm handshake.

Hoping the nerves that were causing his stomach unease were not visible on the outside, Abe shook Milton's hand earnestly.

"I don't have much time before I need to be at the track." Milton was the chairman of the racetrack. He led Abe to his office. "I'm sure you remember our last interaction."

Abe nodded once.

"I can't have trouble on my watch."

Abe nodded again.

"I recognize that you carry yourself differently than your mother. The way you came and rectified the situation right away was impressive. That's the reason I decided to give you a shot in my dining room. I need someone loyal, honest, and sharp under pressure."

Abe's heart rate increased.

"If there's any funny business with any of your family, my decision will be reversed."

Abe shook Milton's hand once more. His nerves were subsiding, and his smile was nothing but genuine after learning that he had been the one chosen to fill the coveted position.

"Welcome to our hotel," Helen Kutsher said. "We conduct our business as if the staff is part of one big extended family." She shook his hand warmly.

"My uncle built the hotel in 1907 and named it the 'Kutsher Brothers Farm House.' It grew and morphed into a powerhouse—always run and maintained as a Jewish resort in the mountains." Milton pointed his feet toward the exit.

Abe's grin could light up all of Sullivan County if the electricity failed.

"The races don't start yet," Helen told her husband with a knowing look. "Wilt called and said to save him a seat at our table on Sunday."

Milton rubbed his hands together gleefully. "He'll be here in time for the Monticello Classic on Monday."

Helen said, "He mentioned Fuzzy Levane wanting to come to take a tour before the Maurice Stokes Benefit Game."

"Go ahead and set that up." Milton turned away from his wife and faced Abe now. "Fuzzy agreed to coach the team opposite Red Auerbach's team."

Fuzzy was the current head coach of the New York Knicks. Abe wondered if anyone in the kitchen would consider toying around with special menu items that pertained to basketball in some way. But at that time, the group of Italians had been outraged to find the Jewish menu had been altered during their stay at the Concord floated through his memory.

"I'm off to see the ponies." Milton trotted out the door like one of the Standardbreds he was en route to watch.

Abe, following closely behind, was ready to tell his nearest and dearest about his exciting new title. Dotty was currently tap dancing, so he hopped in his car and zoomed toward the Concord. Although it had been over a year since he had been co-captain of the staff dining room there, he was going to try to steal some of his trusted staff to join him at Kutsher's.

Aware that Irving would be upset, he also knew the maître d' had tons of people champing at the bit to work for him. He had probably sent away a group of college boys inquiring about work in the dining room earlier that day.

The first person that Abe bumped into at the Concord was Bill Graham. "Any interest in coming over to Kutsher's with me?"

"I'm preparing to move to San Francisco to live near my sister." Bill was beckoned by a bellhop, ending the conversation.

Next, Abe approached a waiter named Bernie, who was a real workhorse. "How'd you like to come over to Kutsher's Country Club and be the captain of my new dining room?"

Bernie beamed at the opportunity and shook Abe's hand to seal the deal.

To Abe's surprise, an aging waiter named Eugene, who had immigrated to the United States after the Hungarian Revolution in 1956, tapped him on the shoulder. "I'll come."

Abe focused his attention on a Morris Katz original painting of a juggling clown. The "King of Toilet Paper Art" had hung the piece on the wall last week. Guests loved it. "Can you believe he uses a palette knife and toilet paper instead of a paintbrush—and all in under five minutes?" Abe was delaying giving Eugene an answer because he had only ever seen him act surly toward guests.

Eugene stared back at him, wrinkles lining his hollow-eyed face. "I have no family. Nowhere to go."

Abe swallowed hard. Eugene was a refugee and that's why Arthur and Irving tolerated his testy attitude, but he did not know the man had no family. Guilt settled in his stomach. "All right," he said, his gut telling him it was the right decision.

He would assign Eugene to the teenager tables. It was the easiest station. Tips were not as good, but the teenagers tended to skip appetizers and soups, and they complained less.

Eugene's gray complexion tugged at Abe's heart some more. He glanced at his watch and had to hoof it home.

Irving, baring his teeth, blocked his path. "Get out of here and leave my staff alone!"

He sprinted down the hill and threw the door open, ready to share his news. "Hello? Anyone home?" Receiving no answer, he went off to share his big news with his best pal.

"*Mazel tov*! I did not expect to keep you as my assistant for long. I'm proud of you. Oh, how far we've come." Leon was gracious as ever. They gave each other a bear hug, both with tears in their eyes.

"Just a couple of mountain rats with the titles of head maître d'." Abe had a smile that could reach Brighton Beach.

CHAPTER 45

DOTTY

Dotty washed down an aspirin with a cool glass of water, trying to prevent a headache. She had to cancel her lesson since cocktails and tap dancing did not mix. She ripped open the bag of peanut M&M's as Abe strutted into the house.

"I got the job!" he announced.

She jumped up. "I'm *kvelling*! How wonderful!" She grew serious. "Your ma better not cause any trouble."

Linda, clad in a pale blue dress, heard the commotion and came fluttering into the kitchen.

"Congratulations, Daddy."

"Thank you, darling." He picked her up and spun her in the air.

Al asked, "Can you introduce me to Wilt?"

"I might be able to arrange that on one of his visits. Even Wilt has to eat." Abe tousled Al's hair. "I've earned a corned beef sandwich on rye with a pickle and potato chips. Leon gave me the night off and we're going to Kaplan's!"

The kids cheered and ran to put on their shoes. "Any excuse for you to eat," Dotty laughed, grabbing her handbag. Her body felt extra warm and cozy from the alcohol she had consumed. It turned out she had been worried for no reason.

Monticello was busy. The storefronts twinkled, and pedestrians were strolling up and down Broadway. The kids begged to go inside the flashy Playland arcade, so they let them play one game each. The line to Kaplan's started at the corner of the block as Abe hustled to join it.

A man in a dark trench coat and a dark fedora swooped by. Dotty shouted out, "Don't lose sight of the children!"

When she glanced over her shoulder, she saw the nefarious-looking man under a streetlamp. Unable to see the front of his face, she shuddered. Missing her step, she rolled her ankle and landed on her *tuchus.*

Abe did not see her fall, but both children ran to her side. They offered their small hands and pulled her into a standing position.

"Are you hurt, Mama?" Linda asked.

She blinked twice. *Was that the mousy woman by the arcade? The same one Mrs. Steingold had mentioned and the same one who had helped her settle that IRS business years ago?* She rubbed her eyes, brushed off her tailored slacks, and composed her balance. "That was silly of me to be so clumsy." She squeezed Linda's warm hand.

Sneaking a peek at the streetlamp behind her, there was no longer any trace of a dark figure lingering underneath. She then kept her eyes on the brightly lit Hebrew National sign above the doorway to Kaplan's as she made her way to join Abe in line.

CHAPTER 46

ABE

Abe kissed Linda on her *keppie* and then softly shut her bedroom door. "Goodnight," he said to Al, who was reading a comic book in his own bedroom.

Dotty had taken another aspirin, and he tucked her into bed. She had been spent from a bender of day drinking and spooked by a man whom she had believed might be the kidnapper from their past.

He assured her that her imagination was running wild and everything would look brighter in the morning. They both knew the fate of ol' D.R. Once her mind was clearer, she would remember the facts.

Relaxing under the carport, gazing up at the stars with a glass of scotch, Leon's new calico kitten, Poppy, was meowing loud enough for him to hear. Leon was smitten and forgave Eva for buying the horse without his consent. If Abe were honest, he would be jealous that he was not also a part-owner of Prince.

"Abey Baby, what's this news I hear through the grapevine? I can't believe I'm staring at the brand-new maître d' of Kutsher's Country Club! How'd you pull it off?"

"I went to an employment agency in the city and told them I was ready for an elite position."

Hershel slapped Abe on the back. "You're the first year-round maître d' they've ever hired! You're a real first-class *gonsa macher*. This is really something else, Abey. You're supervising one of the largest kosher dining rooms in the mountains now. *Mazel tov*! I brought a cigar over to celebrate."

Abe stood there grinning.

Hershel lit the cigar. "You have a special talent for dealing with people and making the little guys feel as if they count. Kutsher's got very lucky." Hershel let Abe have the first puff.

"Have you come to your senses yet? Prince is a good, solid investment. I put down a large amount on him to win the Classic."

"My wife won't approve." He scratched his head, remembering Milton mentioning the Classic.

"You're going to regret it." Hershel blew smoke out of his lips, and Dotty stood in front of the screen door.

"What are you doing up, Dot?" Abe asked.

"I needed a glass of water." She raised her voice. "D.R. might've been on Broadway tonight."

Hershel's posture stiffened. "That's not possible," he stammered.

Suddenly, as if Dotty's mind had cleared, she blurted out, "The skeleton is back in the news."

Abe furrowed his brow. "It's time we find Sy."

"I've been calling all over Atlantic City asking for him. I want to give him the opportunity to be a co-owner of Prince, but I can't find him. I'm getting really worried." Hershel clasped his hands over his head and quickened his breathing.

CHAPTER 47

DOTTY

The week had flown by. The kids were having fun at camp. Abe had completed his employment at the Pines, and Dotty was contemplating joining him at Kutsher's. Her morning coffee mug was in her hand as she breathed the fresh country air.

When Abe snuck up behind her, she shared the idea with him. "All right, Dot. If you're sure, I'll put you on the schedule starting next weekend. You can't leave Leon short for Shabbat dinner."

"I'm sure, Abe. I'll put in my notice tonight." She respected her husband's loyalty to Leon. "Jack Benny is the headliner on Saturday. I'll get one final weekend of working with Eva and seeing a popular comedian there."

Eva sprang through the side door.

"Speak of the devil," Abe said.

Eva shouted, "Prince is winning first place in the Monticello Classic on Monday! I told you it was only a matter of time."

Dotty noticed Abe pause for a moment before speaking in a rather confused tone. "Milton Kutsher mentioned a race on Monday with Wilt Chamberlain traveling to the mountains for it."

Eva clapped her hands together. "Prince will have quite the crowd for his first-place race. Let's play a game of gin rummy at my house."

As Dotty climbed the slight incline, the brightly lit Concord towered in the distance. It evoked a twinge of longing, but she never regretted the move to a smaller-sized resort. She enjoyed working for Leon, who was always fair, but a pang of apprehension tugged at her. *Am I truly ready to hang my apron up at the Pines?*

Sullen about the fact she would no longer work with Eva soon, her feelings seesawed, and she spat out, "We will be wearing different uniforms again." *Achoo.*

Eva paused, shuffling the cards, and removed the cigarette from between her lips. "So, you're going to Kutsher's with Abe?"

Flashing a half-smile, she nodded. "I'll miss you."

"You'll be too busy to miss me much. Besides, we have Mah Jongg every week. We would own a horse together if you and Abe would ante up your share." Eva held her gaze and reached for a manila envelope. "We should invite Rebekah to the next game."

Dotty's eyes bugged out. "Well, what changed your mind?"

"I've realized she's no bimbo. Rebekah wrote this proposal regarding the fashion show and gave it to the rabbi. It's smart and organized."

The calico kitten started meowing. Boychik, sunbathing near the bed of marigolds, purred in his direction.

Dotty did a little tap dancing move. "Might we all be friends after all?"

Chapter 48

Spruced up in a dark gray suit with a bow tie, Abe felt ready for his first Friday night as maître d' of Kutsher's dining room. He was saving his tuxedo for Saturday night, the fanciest dinner of them all. For both breakfast and lunch, he had been competent, in charge, and indebted to his hardworking staff. He was also filled with nervous energy over the fact that one of the two busiest meals of the week was on deck.

He eased into his Chrysler Windsor; perhaps soon he could purchase the black Buick Roadmaster sedan he had been eyeing. They were nearly done paying off their car loan. It still stung when he thought about how they had intended to pay it off years ago.

After parking in his assigned spot, he rolled his neck around and took a couple of deep breaths, wondering if he would ever get used to seeing his name written on the sign stuck in the ground in front of him. He saluted the security guard, said hello to a bellhop, and took the path that wound through the lobby decorated with orange, green, and cream-colored chairs. Jazz music wafted through the air.

Filled with pride, observing every table in the banquet setting, the pressure of manning it all was enormous. The dining room was similar in size to the one he had just come from, seating about four hundred people. However, there was no separate staff dining room at Kutsher's like there was at both the Concord and the Pines.

He reviewed the seating chart. It was his responsibility to make every guest feel like a VIP and seat the true VIPs at the most prominent locations. There was a hierarchical system. It did take a great amount of skill and forethought. The order was of utmost importance. Pleasing a roomful of hungry guests and ensuring that tablemates would get along was not the easiest task. The ultimate luxury for guests was thinking they had been given access to a special table or a special order, and the compensation for masterminding that was usually monetary.

On his own, he started dragging tables. He was panting by the time his staff began to trickle in. A good handful of them were college boys on their summer breaks, wearing their white jackets with gold on the lapel. They knew what they were doing and hastily prepared for a busy meal.

A waiter asked to speak to him. "I'd like a certain station where the crème de la crème sits." He handed Abe a decent tip to lock it down before dashing off to gather the livestock.

Guests would soon stampede into the room in their dazzling outfits. It was sports jackets for men and evening gowns for women. In no time at all, dinner was seemingly off to the races.

Milton shook his hand kindly. "*Shabbat Shalom.* Welcome aboard," he said, and then claimed his spot at the Kutsher family table. Every white-clothed table in the dining room had red wine, challah, and Shabbos candles set out.

Abe made a beeline over to Joe Lapchick, a member of the Original Celtics, former New York Knicks head coach, and the current head coach of St.

John's University.

"I heard there's a new maître d'. It's a pleasure to meet you. Kutsher's is the best hotel in the mountains." Joe stuck out his hand. He was there on vacation for several weeks.

Abe returned his firm handshake. "I'm happy to be here."

Trays stacked with Friday night entrées balanced on raised arms rushed by. The dining room was in full throttle. Abe took a moment to step back and observe it all. The food presentation, with tasteful garnishes, looked both sophisticated and homey. There was a robust mix of couples and singles from Brooklyn, Queens, Manhattan, Long Island, Westchester, and New Jersey.

He searched the room for the single fella who had requested to sit at the most sought-after table. Abe had pocketed the crisp dollar bills and led the way to a table full of VIPs. Now he located the guest talking to a gal at the table behind him. He had an inclination that he would want to switch to that table for the next meal.

A bellhop was jogging right through the room. "You have a phone call in the office."

"I'm busy. Whoever it is can wait. Take a message."

"They're really serious that I must get you on the other end."

Abe spun around, taking sight of every angle of the dining room. He recalled what Dotty had blurted out during a stupor last week about the skeleton being back in the news. He had presumed she had forgotten she had mentioned it because she had not brought it up again. And he had not heard anything in the news himself. But still, he became ill at ease. He raced after the bellhop. "Hello!" he yelled into the phone.

"Abe-*ala,* you forgot to tell your mother about your new job. I had to hear it from your sister."

"Ma, I'm a busy man in charge of a lot of staff."

"Summer sun and winter fun," Ma said in a singsong voice, repeating the latest advertisement Kutsher's had created.

"I don't have time for this right now."

"Fine. I'll travel to the mountains for the High Holidays."

Click. Abe slammed the receiver down without a goodbye and charged back to the dining room. He rubbed his temples, recalling Jean telling him Papa wanted to spend the High Holidays in the mountains as well. He could not bear having a repeat experience like the one at the Concord when he had first started. Ma had shown up with Jean, then Papa had also checked in for the weekend. During one of the meals, Ma had thrown a pumpernickel roll at Papa's head, with the entire dining room gawking. *Oy vey, the embarrassment of it all.*

The idea of Ma back at Kutsher's was atrocious. He did not want his boss reversing his decision to hire him. Milton had threatened it as a real possibility if any funny business with Ma occurred.

Abe straightened his glasses and jumped with two feet back into the rhythm of the dining room. He checked in on Coach Lapchick. The skilled coach was shoveling broiled ribeye into his mouth like it was the last meal he would ever eat. Kutsher's had a butcher in-house, and Abe could tell the cut of the night was superior.

"Wilt will be here to see Rival Time take first place in the Classic over at the track," Milton told his 12-top.

Helen, sitting to his left, said, "Isn't it exciting!"

Abe stopped mid-strut, crossing his fingers that he had heard wrong. "Is that so?" he heard Joe ask.

"Sure is," said Milton, prematurely smiling triumphantly.

Abe grew confused. He had thought the top honor on Monday belonged to Prince. That's what Hershel had said. There must have been a mix-up in communication somewhere along the way—Hershel made a substantial bet on the race. His heart rate was as fast as if he were running a race himself.

Crash! A plate smashing to the ground caught his attention. Eugene, the refugee who had relocated from the Concord, cut his thumb. Abe steered him to where they kept the first aid kit while simultaneously signaling to a busboy to leap into action and check on Eugene's station. Another busboy was already sweeping up the broken plate.

Abe unwrapped a Band-Aid and gently bandaged Eugene's thumb. He knew this pain was nothing compared to losing his family. For a variety of complicated reasons, the Holocaust was hardly ever discussed openly among Jews, even among survivors.

The hecticness of the dining room could not be ignored, so Abe had no choice but to send Eugene back to his duties.

Presently, he had to turn his attention to two guests bickering because one had convinced the other to order spinach soup, and that guest was unhappy with the choice. "Let me remind you that you can order as many bowls of soup as you'd like," Abe said.

"She already ordered the cold fruit soup, the matzo ball soup, and the split pea soup. How much soup does a person need?" asked the disgruntled guest.

"My coffee isn't hot enough," complained another guest.

Abe directed the busboy he caught bent over a serving tray scarfing down food to "go place an empty cup upside down on the griddle." It was a trick to make the guests believe their coffee was even hotter.

He would not allow his staff to go around eating whatever they felt like at any given moment, even though he realized it was a regular occurrence. He grabbed the closest busboy and said, "Call over to the Laurels and tell Hershel I need to speak to him right away."

"I need to speak to you right away," said a lanky man with a Brooklyn accent and a Dodgers baseball cap on his head. An FBI badge was in his hand.

He looks familiar. Abe narrowed his eyes.

"The last time you saw me, I was wearing a cowboy hat and using a fake country accent."

Chapter 49

DOTTY

"There's bad news," Dotty overheard Phil Shwied tell his wife. She strained to hear the rest of the conversation. It was her last Friday night at the Pines. Neither Leon nor Eva had been one bit surprised to hear she was following Abe to Kutsher's.

"Joe DiMaggio canceled."

Mae, with an armful of bread, shook a bialy in the air. "Who will fill in at the last minute?"

Knowing this would put the guests in grumpy moods, Dotty became sluggish. She had been hoping to be the one to come home with an autograph for Al tonight. Joe DiMaggio was scheduled to run a clinic the first night of his two-week vacation in the mountains. Now the popular ex-Yankee center fielder's arrival was delayed.

The news traveled throughout the dining room. One guest glumly said, "I tried to style my hair exactly like Marilyn Monroe's so Joe would notice me."

"I wore my best dress," said the girl across from her.

Dotty found Leon and advised him to send over a plate of assorted butter cookies and coconut cake to mend their unhappy hearts.

"I came here under the impression that I was meeting a baseball player, so they should find another baseball player," said a crotchety *alta cocker*, in between spooning prune whip into his mouth.

"Oh, you think it's so easy, Seymour. What? You

expect Yankee players to be walking around the mountains a dime a dozen with nothing to do." His wife viciously bit into her macaroon.

Dotty turned to the 10-top filled with a group of nurses who had traveled together during the war. They were hosting a reunion at the Pines. For breakfast, they had ordered grapefruit and melons. For lunch, they had stuck with salads. Now they were voraciously hungry for dinner, devouring hearty plates of apricot chicken and lamb shoulder chops.

A guest began to groan gravely. Dotty was grateful there were nurses nearby. Within seconds, Eva was handing her a mixture of prune juice and hot water with a squeeze of lemon inside a milkshake glass and whispering in her ear, "Mountain magic, guaranteed to make the guest no longer feel impacted."

After the guest drank it all down, miraculously, the impaction did vanish. Dotty said a big "thank you" to Eva, and a pang ran through her gut. Soon, her dear friend would not be able to back her up in times like this.

"Don't give away the secret at Kutsher's." Eva bumped into her with her shoulder.

The activity director's voice boomed over the loudspeaker. The dining room grew quiet. Everyone was curious to hear what was so important. "There's been a special surprise added to tonight's lineup." He paused to let the anticipation grow. "There will be a talent show with two athletes performing!"

The guests were skeptical. The activity director continued, "Sonny Liston and Joe Frazier will get the show started!"

The dining hall came to life—guests fluffed their

hair and sat up taller, impatient for the rest of the evening once again. They might not be going home with Joe DiMaggio autographs, but they would be going home with famed professional boxers' signatures instead.

Dotty overheard one guest say, "Joe Shmoe, I don't even remember who that guy is."

"That's because you're a Dodgers fan!" shouted the guest to his right.

It was a real stroke of good luck that both boxers were training at the Pines for their next matches. She would get her work done and then go stand in the back to watch.

As she took off her apron, exhaustion settled into her feet. Nostalgia for her last weekend at the Pines filled her heart.

Hershel burst through the door. He spat out, "Milton Kutsher and Wilt Chamberlain are scheming to fix Monday's race in Rival Time's favor."

Eva's eyes grew fiery. "Prince is winning."

Hershel stomped his feet emphatically. "That's right. They can't go fixing it another way. It's already been set."

Dotty remained tight-lipped. It was a particularly tough spot to be caught in, with Milton being Abe's boss.

"You must go in on the horse!" Eva cried.

"We can't afford it," Dotty said.

***

"Dot!" Abe came running into the house. "Remember the Oklahoma oilman?"

"Yes, the man in charge of the Bad Investment in 1954."

"He's no southerner; he's from Brooklyn." Abe handed Dotty an envelope.

Her jaw dropped. She read the note and lifted the check from the envelope, rereading it over and over.

Her thoughts raced. "How can we be so lucky? The promotion, and we got our money back."

He repeated it two more times.

"Pinch me!" she squealed.

He playfully pinched her and said, "Our pockets are full of cash again."

She giggled into his ear and looked at the check once more. "We can buy the horse now."

CHAPTER 50

ABE

Still astonished, Abe proudly wore his tuxedo on Saturday evening, strutting by cosmetic counters, jewelry displays, and art showcases. The on-site beauty parlor was booked with reservations, just one of many indications that it was going to be nonstop action all night long.

He burst through the kitchen doors in a tough-guy boss persona. "What's good back here?" he asked the cooks, inhaling the rich aromas from all different directions. He liked to be prepared with suggestions when a guest asked him for help deciding what to order.

"The broiled salmon is very fresh," said the dining room steward. "It was delivered this morning."

"What kind of fish is in the kugel?"

"It's a canned flake fish," hollered a bimmy who had been sober enough for the last two nights to act as third cook.

"I expect the calf brain to be a top pick," said the chef.

"Don't forget to remove it." Abe gestured at the metal plumba tag clamped to a chicken thigh, identifying the poultry as kosher. He could not have another incident like the toothpick one with the Bergs at the Concord occurring on his watch. It had been his first morning carrying tables of his own as a waiter when a toothpick fell into a bowl of oatmeal by accident. Luckily, the activity director had come to his rescue, offering a free bottle of wine, fibbing that they had been playing a game to see who could find the toothpick.

Now he studied the French verbiage on the dinner menu and proceeded to read over the desserts next. Along with an in-house butcher, there was a renowned baker. He imagined the heavenly scent of the orange sponge cake that was baking in the oven, coaxing guests right out of their rooms and directly into the dining room.

Carefully arranging the seating chart, he worried that he did not have enough staff to cover all the stations tonight, so he even hired the busboy that Hershel informed him provided shoddy service. As long as he did not drop unpleasant comments to the guests, any extra hands on deck would be helpful. Envious that Leon had both Dotty and Eva carrying stations under his watch, he adjusted his tuxedo jacket, anticipating it would be a whirlwind on a sold-out Saturday night. He was ready to oversee that every guest, decked out in their required black tie for men and evening gowns for women, was comfortable and well-fed.

Milton Kutsher appeared. The big boss was wiping his forehead with a handkerchief and leading a group of men.

Abe stepped forward to guide the dapper gentlemen to their requested 8-top in the dimmest corner of the room. Milton exchanged words with the stockiest one. The only part of the conversation that Abe was able to hear clearly was the name Rival Time. Relieved that Dotty was not here—she would have been preoccupied with concern that the table of men was associates of Drucker's—he, on the other hand, found them to be very friendly. He would keep a heavy focus on their corner for the duration of their dining experience.

He watched his staff weaving around the tables, delivering massive trays of food. The dining room sparkled from all the fancy jewels layered on exquisite attire. As predicted, the calf brain appetizer was a hit. However, the fish kugel was only given a lukewarm review.

A waitress was wailing about being out of soup spoons and growing increasingly agitated over her need for more, all the while gesturing at Eugene, blaming him for stealing all her spoons. The busboy that Hershel had warned him against came to her assistance while Eugene kept his head low and muttered to himself. Abe made a note in his mind to compliment the busboy later and to set some time aside to speak with his staff about what Eugene had been through and why he was so surly.

He noticed a waiter carrying a plate of fish kugel over to one of the dapper gentlemen. "Here, I'll take that." Immediately, he chucked it into the garbage, replacing it with an order of broiled salmon. He also grabbed bottles of scotch and bourbon.

"Order more food. One entrée isn't enough around here." Abe set the broiled salmon down in front of a man wearing a chunky brass pinky ring. For several seconds, as he filled each of their glasses, D.R.'s ring, which looked identical in his memory to this one, lingered in his mind.

His subtle attentiveness was appreciated by the dapper gentlemen, as evident from their generous tips. Compensation like that, alongside their polite tones, well, he would not mind them stopping by again soon.

Abe was both wound up with energy and

exhausted by the time the orange sponge cake was devoured, and a mass exodus took place. On Saturdays, just like at the Concord and the Pines, guests bulldozed their way out of the dining room, hustling to the nightclub. A new young comedian named Mal Z. Lawrence was putting on his act inside the Deep End Lounge, and everyone wanted to get the best seat.

He applauded his staff: "Job well done! Tonight was a good meal."

"How many guests will walk out of the show?" a busboy asked.

"A bunch of *putzes*," said another busboy.

"Let them have their fun," a waitress said.

The dining room steward added, "Maybe everybody will be mesmerized by Mal Z."

Abe listened to the chatter of his staff as his eyes scanned the room that had been prepared for the high-energy breakfast crowd that would spill through the doors, demanding juice and danishes in the morning. He nodded in approval at the tidy tables covered in clean, white tablecloths.

He had seen Eugene exit dinner as soon as the guests finished their desserts, so he was not currently in attendance. Abe cleared his throat. "I'd like you all to make an extra-special effort to be kind to Eugene."

"He's miserable. He won't talk to anyone other than the guests he serves, and even then, he grunts in monosyllables," said a busboy.

"Have you noticed he shows up in the dining room 15 minutes before the guests and leaves the second the meal ends?" asked a waitress.

"I've only heard him growl or snort. He locks himself in his room with his broken-down television every free second that he has. He wants nothing to do with us," said a waiter.

"His TV is on its last legs," confirmed another busboy.

Abe took a deep breath and let it out slowly before sharing, "Eugene lost all his family during the Holocaust. He deserves to be cut a break."

Bernie, the captain of the dining room, jumped into action. "I'm starting a donation right this second. Who wants to contribute to a brand-new television for Eugene?"

Cash came flying out of pockets. Abe emptied some of his wallet into the fund as his heart swelled with pride over his staff's kindness.

Assured that Eugene would be treated kindly, Abe moved on to inspecting the armful of clothing given to him by a designer from Manhattan. He picked up a pair of black leather shoes and inspected the sole. The designer had requested the best table in the room. Abe had thanked him for his generosity and sat him directly next to a stunning actress who had starred in several Broadway shows. He put the shoes down, finished his duties, and vacated the dining room.

With a wide grin that resembled the half-moon gleaming in the night sky, he reached his assigned parking spot.

A hand clasped his left shoulder. Locking eyes with Hershel, he recognized right away that his friend was in a riled-up state.

"Tell your boss that Prince is winning. It's not Rival Time's race to win, Abey."

He raised his hands in self-defense. "I can't lose my job. I think I should back out."

"Too late, Abey, I already handed over the money you gave me this morning. You're officially an owner." Shaking his fists in the air and saying a string of incoherent Yiddish words, he stormed off, leaving Abe fumbling with his keys.

Chapter 51

DOTTY

Dotty was still riding the high from learning they were getting all their money back. She remembered that last night, Abe had been bothered by a visit from Hershel. It seemed Hershel was refusing to let the race be fixed in Rival Time's favor no matter what. She pulled at her apron strings.

It was rather common knowledge that the betting was crooked, and that fixed racing was a regular occurrence. Owners, drivers, and trainers would meet at a popular restaurant hangout and decide over a burger who would push and who would hold back. Usually, two to three drivers in a race helped each other out, blocking and boxing accordingly.

Guests pushed through the doors. Feeding them and collecting tips kept her mind centered on nothing but the tasks at hand.

"Who else will be able to convince the cook to combine buttermilk and blue cheese to make my coleslaw?" asked a picky guest who handed Dotty a couple of crisp bills.

"Request to sit at Eva's table." She winked and pocketed the generous tip. Having grown to look forward to *schmoozing* with this guest every weekend of her six-week stay, she became overcome with emotion and dabbed at her eyes with a napkin.

"I heard Mal Z. Lawrence is already booked back at Kutsher's for his second performance. Now you'll get to see his next show," said another guest, who had his fist wrapped around her cash tip. She had grown fond of him as well.

When the meal was over, Eva caught up to her. "You are my favorite waitress to work alongside, and nothing will change that. If you ever get fed up with working at Kutsher's, come back over here."

Dotty wiped the corners of her eyes again. In private, she would fill Eva in on everything with the oilman later. "Abe paid our share for Prince after breakfast."

Eva threw her arms around Dotty's neck. "You came to your senses! We can still catch a race tonight. I'm going to the track; are you coming? Stakes are high these days."

Spent from her last weekend at the Pines, Dotty could not imagine having the energy to sit at the track right now. Prince was not racing, and her house in Kiamesha was the only place she longed to be. She took one last scan of the Pines dining room; her eyes landed on an in-demand Leon, who was unaware of any upcoming turbulence. "I'm going home."

Eva was off in a flash.

Confident she would return soon for one reason or another, instead of sadness, she let excitement for a new adventure at Kutsher's settle over her.

At home, her hands flew to her chest when she read the message that Clem had scribbled down. It said that Sy had called with news that had not been released to the public yet. She locked the door, something that was never done in the middle of the day. *Was this what the man at the bowling alley had been alluding to?*

Not long after that, Abe was banging his fist on

the door. "Why'd you lock it, Dot?"

"Sy called—you need to call him back right away."

"Did he leave a number?"

"Right here," she showed him the message.

He went directly to the rotary phone and started dialing. "Hello, can I please speak with Sy. Well okay, I'll call back in a couple of hours."

"He wasn't there?"

"No, but the man said to call back, and he might have more information for me later."

"You must call back!"

"I will." Abe tossed an envelope full of his 'birthday notes' onto the dining room table. "Maybe he was calling to congratulate us on gaining our investment money back."

Dotty picked the envelope up, impressed by its weight. "You'd better put it in the safe."

"That's what I intend to do." Abe shared a story from the morning. "A family snuck out of breakfast without tipping, so I had a couple of busboys surround their car. Come to find out, they have not been tipping for years. They threw so much money out the window that if they never tip again, nobody will complain."

She handed the envelope back to him, glad to hear that, in the end, nobody was stiffed a tip.

"I'm planning on getting Wilt's autograph for Al tomorrow."

"He'll be tickled."

The reason why Wilt would be at Kutsher's hung heavily in the room.

Abe pulled out a chair. "Dot, I'd never bet against Prince or our friends if it weren't my job at stake."

"You can't lose your job. There will be other races for Prince to win." She ripped open a bag of peanut M&M's, counting the possible reasons why Sy would call out of the blue with news. When her mind flitted from worry over the racetrack situation to dread over the skeleton, she tossed the empty candy wrapper into the trash can and lit the last Lucky Strike in her pack.

CHAPTER 52

ABE

Swinging his driver at hole number one and breathing in fresh mountain air on the front nine of the golf course, Abe was releasing the tension he had built up during mealtime. The pressure was extreme, but his days as a whole were enjoyable, and he liked going to work, which was a good thing since he worked all seven days of the week.

The mountains were the place to be. Lucille Ball was the headliner at the Concord. Alan King was performing at the Pines, and the biggest basketball game ever to be played in the mountains was fast approaching.

He trekked off the golf course and called Sy again. It rang five times before a different man than the one he had previously spoken with answered, and it took another five minutes for him to locate a note that said Sy was on his way to help some old friends in upstate New York somewhere. Abe called the Laurels. As he waited while the operator sent a bellhop to locate Hershel, he realized that he really did not have much time to wait around, so he hung up and charged back to the dining room.

Earlier he had learned that a Rabbinical Assembly was being held a week after the Stokes game. It was urgent that he sort through a stack of applications to ensure that there would be enough staff to feed all the guests in attendance at both events.

Kutsher's did not have a union. Only the Concord

and Grossinger's did. He was reading over the experience list, intending to give more than the "politicals" a home in his dining room when a boy of about 18 years old, spiffed up in slacks and a button-down shirt, interrupted him with his hand extended.

"Do you have a minute?"

Curiosity piqued, he laid the applications aside, shook the kid's hand, and liked that the greeting was firm and confident.

"I'm Ira. A mutual acquaintance told me you might have a job available for me. I want to save money for school."

"What are you studying?" Abe liked that Ira was a straight arrow.

"Medicine. I want to be a surgeon one day."

"Have you ever worked around food?"

"No. I assure you that I'm a fast learner."

"Who's the mutual acquaintance?"

"Lebel Winchinsky, the bread delivery man."

Abe got a kick out of the connection. "I guess we'd better get you set up carving the ribeye. You'll need the experience for all the surgeries you're going to perform." It just so happened to be Sunday, and every Sunday, ribeye was served for dinner at Kutsher's.

The boy grew sheepish. "Do you think you can hire my younger brother? He's studying to be a lawyer, and he's a hard worker. I can vouch for him."

Admiring the kid's *chutzpah,* he decided to hire his brother sight unseen. "I'll call you Brother Number One and Brother Number Two."

Ira bowed in appreciation and vacated the dining room.

Not a second later, Hershel came barreling

through the entryway. "How's my favorite maître d' in the mountains?"

"I'm still standing." Abe remembered their last interaction the night before and was relieved that Hershel was calmer today. He watched the door, worried that Milton would show up and learn that Abe was involved with the horse competing against Rival Time.

"Attaboy. Now let's go see some jewelry." Hershel bashfully ran a hand through his jet-black hair, which had the same thickness as the day Abe had met him.

Abe squinted his eyes at his pal.

"It's time I purchase an engagement ring."

Abe's eyebrows shot toward the ceiling. "*Mazel tov!*"

They swiftly strutted to the twinkling jewelry store located inside Kutsher's. A steady stream of guests admired the cases of sparkling gems.

"Business is booming," the jeweler said.

"It's about to get a lot better. I want to purchase an engagement ring," Hershel said.

"I have the perfect one." The jeweler fiddled with his key ring to unlock the glass case.

Hershel smacked his palm against his forehead. "Abey, it's a necklace like the one stolen from Eva! I must buy it for her."

No clear recollection of what Eva's necklace had looked like; he thought this opal-shaped heart, encrusted in white gold and hanging from a delicate chain, was beautiful. He also thought Leon ought to be the one to make the purchase for his wife.

The jeweler swung his arms and removed it from

the case. "I only have two of these gorgeous gems in stock."

Hershel grabbed the necklace and held it up to the light. "It's so similar." His radiant smile was brighter than all the diamonds on display.

The jeweler tapped his knuckle near the cushion-cut, three-carat diamond engagement ring.

"It's exquisite. Wrap that up for me as well," said Hershel.

Abe nearly lost his breath, imagining how much it cost. It was a risky purchase since the betting on Prince would not come through.

The jeweler's grin had never been bigger. "The recipient must be very special."

Hershel winked. "They both are."

Abe glanced sideways. The jeweler coyly placed his hand over his mouth.

"You see, the opal necklace is for a gal who will always be very special to me, but I'm moving on for good. The engagement ring is for the gal who owns my heart now."

CHAPTER 53

DOTTY

"Will you call the doctor today and schedule a physical, Abe?"

"Yes, dear." He kissed her on the cheek.

"And try to contact Sy?" Dying to learn what his message meant, she bit her bottom lip.

"Yes, dear," he said again, shuffling through some business cards to find the doctor's number.

Dotty rinsed her coffee mug in the sink. "Surely Hershel came to his senses and isn't challenging the race being fixed in Rival Time's favor anymore?"

"He's determined to stick with Prince."

She saw the defeat in her husband's eyes, knowing he had no other choice but to root against their own horse if he wanted to remain maître d' of Kutsher's Country Club. She put her arms around his waist and gave him a squeeze goodbye.

About an hour later, she noticed Abe had left the doctor's business card on the kitchen table. She took matters into her own hands and held the rotary receiver up to her ear. "Can I please speak to the doctor?"

"That's not possible. He's a busy man," said the stern receptionist.

"Well, can I schedule an appointment for my husband, please?"

"Give me your name and phone number, and if it's possible to fit you in sometime this year, I'll contact you."

Dotty did as she was told, even though she felt

like she was being reprimanded in school for doing something she was unaware of.

The receptionist repeated his name aloud, and instantaneously, the doctor's voice was on the other end of the line. "Congratulations on Abe's new position! Milton and Helen Kutsher are personal friends. For the head maître d' of my favorite resort, I have room. I'll rearrange my schedule. How's Thursday afternoon? Just make sure he seats me at the VIP table near Milton next time I eat at Kutsher's."

She placed the rotary receiver on the cradle and sprayed a little Chantilly perfume on her wrists. It was time to drop the kids off at camp.

"Vinny Perlstein hit two home runs the last time we played softball," Al said as they drove down the mountain.

"Terrific!" said Dotty. She was fond of little Vinny, who was already the tallest child enrolled in the Heiden day camp.

"He told me he'd practice with me today."

"I don't want to play softball," said Linda.

"You don't have to," Dotty told her.

She left the kids in the hands of their teenage counselors, who wore red t-shirts paired with white baseball caps and smiles full of gumption. Then she drove the two minutes to her parents' bungalow. They were visiting friends staying at the Tamarack Lodge, but she wanted to leave the doctor's name on a note for Ma. Papa could use a proper check-up. She scribbled to mention Abe's name if the irritable receptionist tried to say there was no availability.

The screen door rattled behind her as she saw the mousy clerk from the courthouse. The other night near

Kaplan's, she had been able to convince herself it had only been a delusion that she had seen the same woman. There's no denying it now. She swallowed hard.

"Hello, I'm Hannah. Is Dotty here?" the clerk asked Rose Levner, who was *schlepping* a mattress on her back.

"A second ago, I saw her over there." Rose jutted the left side of her body toward Dotty's parents' bungalow.

Dotty hitched her breath. It was time for a grand entrance. "Hello, I'm here."

Hannah walked closer and flitted her eyes toward the sky. "I finally have the courage to speak to you."

Rose informed them, "Bingo is inside the casino after dinner," while dragging the mattress on her back in the direction of the two-bedroom bungalow where the pair of usually feisty Shih Tzus were all tuckered out on the lawn.

"My parents aren't home. We can use their porch."

Hannah nodded and followed Dotty through the grass.

"Here, sit." She moved an issue of *National Geographic* from the worn wicker rocker. "Would you like a cup of tea?"

Hannah shook her head "no" and sat on the edge of the rocking chair, so her feet rested on the ground. "It's time I admit who I am."

Dotty wondered if she should quickly grab the letter opener she saw on Papa's table. Hannah's trembling limbs gave her confidence that she was not in physical danger, though. She hurried to rip open a pack of Lucky Strikes and lit a match.

Hannah kept her eyes on the ceiling. "My mother and father adopted my brother from an orphanage when he was eighteen months old. My mom desperately wanted a baby. I came along a decade later, long after my mom ever thought she would have a biological child." Hannah kept talking as if she had to get everything out all at once, "Mother told me Joel became rebellious around the age of 11."

Who is Joel?

"By the time he was 13, my parents were at their wits' end and sent him to be an assistant milker at the Breezy Hill Farm House up here. My dad's cousins owned it. They all hoped getting Joel out of the city and teaching him a trade would straighten his behavior out."

"Joel?" Dotty said out loud this time. She looked at the time.

"That's the name my parents gave him when they adopted him. The D.R. nonsense was not what any of us called him any day of his life."

"D.R.," Dotty stammered.

"Little did anyone expect that because he was up here, he would run into Jack Drucker and an organization as sinister as Murder, Inc. Well, that's what happened. He was so young that even Drucker tried to get him off his back, but Joel was relentless. He managed to get himself a role in the slot machine business in the mountains."

"I need tea," Dotty said, hurrying to the kitchen. She leaned over the sink to compose herself. Several minutes later, she returned with cups of peppermint tea resting on saucers. "Were you close to your brother?"

Hannah took hold of a teacup and grimaced. "Not at all. No matter what opportunity my parents gave him, he would make a mess of it. He was adopted into a loving family. To the day both of my parents took their last breaths, they supported him and were willing to give him another chance."

Dotty sipped her tea. "Do you have any idea what became of him?" She was praying she sounded naive.

Hannah took a deep inhale and held the air in her lungs before releasing it. "That's the real reason I'm here." She stared down at her teacup. "I knew Joel or D.R. or whatever you want to call him was up to no good, but I also had a trip planned that I had been looking forward to for a long time. So, I ignored my intuition and sent Mother to stay at the Concord with him for a week. In my wildest dreams, I would've never imagined she was capable of burning down the nightclub because she was feeding a stray cat and then ending up in the hospital."

Dotty recalled that crazy time. The teacup wobbled in her hand.

"I checked Mother out of the hospital and followed Joel up to Rochester. Mother begged me to. We knew he had a place up there." Hannah dropped her head. "I found material from your ripped evening gown. I felt terrible that you and Abe were involved."

Dotty cringed, remembering the car ride to Rochester and the cubbyhole that she and Abe had been forced into. Her gown was in shreds by the end of the ordeal.

"I gave Mother her sleeping pills so she would stay in the car while I figured out what in the world I was supposed to do next when I saw Joel's lifeless body in a wheelbarrow half-submerged in the creek."

Dotty looked for a nearby handkerchief in case

Hannah needed it.

"To be completely honest, I was relieved. My brother's reign of terror was over for good."

Dotty understood that, but she had lots of questions that she started firing off. "Are those his bones in the courthouse? Did you put them there? What happened to the safe with the rest of the money?"

Hannah's shaky voice rose an octave. "I brought Joel's body home and buried him in Mother's yard. Mother never knew. When she woke up back in Monticello, I told her Joel was spending time in Canada for a while to lay low. I don't think she truly believed it, but she wanted to, so she did. After she died and her house had to be sold, I dug up his bones and put them in the box that the electrician uncovered. I didn't know what to do with them and panicked one day, stuffing them into the room at the courthouse. It was a twist of fate that the 1944 stamp happened to be on the box. I bought my own lock and threw away the key. As for the money, I donated every penny to charity. Some to the Monticello Hospital, more to the local animal shelter, and the rest to several different orphanages." She coughed into her hand. "If I donated that amount of money to only one location, I was bound to receive unwanted attention."

Dotty clanked her teacup down onto the saucer, thinking those were appropriate benefactors. She squinted at Hannah's petite body. *There was no way she buried D.R. alone.* "Did you have help?"

Hannah dropped her chin to her chest and whispered, "Sy," so softly that Dotty was not entirely sure the woman had actually spoken at all. But Dotty also knew that if anyone helped clean up the mess with no fanfare, it had to be Sy.

Hannah was scooting toward the door. "I wanted to tell you for so long. I tried, but I always chickened out. Now it's like Mother is guiding me from the grave to be courageous."

"Come to the Pines on the weekend and I'll make sure you get a delicious meal." Dotty was realizing that the mysterious shadows over the years now had a solid explanation.

"I'm moving to Connecticut next week. I wanted all of this off my chest before I go. Once again, I apologize for how my brother's behavior affected you a decade ago. You didn't deserve his wrath."

"Do you want his ring back?"

Hannah's voice was little more than a whisper. "He thought that ring made him look so powerful." She scrunched up her nose. "No, I don't want it. I threw it as far as I could into the creek; how did it end up with you?"

The Oklahoma oilman had told Abe that a silly little cat kept swiping evidence out of his bag when he was at the Concord. They had chuckled over Boychik being a real-life cat burglar—he had stolen the ring, the torn emerald-green fabric, and the Rochester house photograph.

Hannah did not wait for an answer; she was halfway out the door already. Dotty darted her eyes to the fishing pole in the corner—the one Al had given to her father from the donations to the Cub Scouts. The one she had just now learned was originally D.R.'s. She waved a gentle goodbye and grabbed her car keys.

***

Dotty dug D.R.'s chunky brass pinky ring from her

dresser drawer and hustled over to Kiamesha Lake. She imagined herself pitching in a softball game with Al and his friends while throwing the ring as far as she could. She watched the splash, heard an osprey whistle overhead, and then hurried back to Eva's house.

"You're in the nick of time." Eva pushed a loose curl under her taupe scarf that she wore to drive.

Dotty opened the passenger door of the white Chevrolet. She sat rigid in semi-shock over what Hannah had revealed. She needed to tell Abe. "Turn on the radio," she requested, surmising that a news program would be a smart way to listen for clues as to why Sy had called.

Ten minutes later, Dotty asked, "Are you sure you took the correct turn?"

Eva nodded that she had followed directions. "Rebekah said the wig shop is no more than a quarter of a mile past a red barn with two silos, but there are no silos in sight." She slammed on the gas.

"We need to arrive in one piece!" Dotty hollered. In five minutes, they were supposed to meet with a woman who was donating wigs for the fashion show.

"Uh oh," Eva said as the car sputtered, and the radio host made an announcement.

"Folks, we have an update on a story we've been following for quite some time. The skeleton found inside the hidden room at the courthouse is finally undergoing a forensic examination. Results are forthcoming from the district attorney's office."

One hand flew to cover Dotty's mouth while the other covered her heart. She remained frozen as the car stalled.

In short order, Eva was out of the car. She popped

the trunk and fiddled with something under the hood. "I'll jog to a gas station." She began stretching her calf muscles.

"That could be miles," Dotty worried, wiggling out of the overheated vehicle. She scanned their surroundings—nothing but the forest.

"We must take action into our own hands. We can't miss Prince winning."

"We won't because the race is fixed for Rival Time."

Eva stopped rolling her ankles around and kicked dirt in Dotty's direction. "Prince is winning."

Dotty took a couple of big steps backward while she searched for motorists and listened for engines.

"Leon thinks Rival Time should win just like you and Abe." Eva was digging her heels into the dirt.

Dotty appreciated Leon's loyalty, never doubting it for a moment. A car was driving their way. She jumped into the air, waving her arms.

"All three of you are chickens." Eva lunged and screeched, "Stop!" at the car as it neared.

The car slowed but kept going forward. "I have to drop the newspapers off. I'm late! I'll send help," the driver yelled.

Eva kicked more dirt. Two fawns scampered by. Dotty continued to pray for a safe rescue while fanning herself with her hands. They were missing their appointment at the wig shop. The trifecta of bickering with Eva, the skeleton announcement, and Hannah's confession on top of the direct sun beating down made her sick to her stomach.

CHAPTER 54

ABE

Brother Number One, the elder brother of what he had coined the Brother Team, was smoking a cigarette and pouring water. Abe liked pulling the brothers' legs as much as he could tell they enjoyed pulling his. Brother Number One was trying to provoke him. Abe pretended not to know and yelled dramatically but not seriously angry, "You know the rules: no smoking in the dining room. After lunch, you're done—outta my dining room for the rest of the summer!"

Amid their first meal, he had watched them skillfully assist the waitresses they were assigned to with chivalry. It was also impressive how much weight they could carry on one tray. These were the types of team players he wanted working for him.

Today he was giving them each one of the best stations simply because they were so competent. Still, he gave them a stern gaze that sent them skedaddling to the opposite side of the dining room.

The captain of the dining room came to his side and held an envelope in his hand. Cupping his hand over his mouth, he hollered toward Eugene, "We have something for you."

Eugene stopped to pick up a piece of lint off the floor, then to adjust his apron, next to tie his shoe, and then, finally, he made his way over.

"On behalf of everyone." The captain thrust the envelope into Eugene's hands and circled his arms around the entire dining room.

Eugene stared at the envelope. His eyes narrowed. "For me?"

"To buy yourself a brand-new TV."

Eugene's forehead furrowed. "For me?" he repeated.

Abe blurted out, "So you can enjoy your free time much better." He left out any part of Eugene's background so as not to make him feel that they pitied him.

Eugene tore open the envelope, saw the stack of cash, and burst into "Thank you!" so loudly that Abe nearly pinched himself to make sure he was not imagining things.

"This is the nicest thing anyone has done for me since I lost my family." Eugene clutched the envelope to his chest before slipping it snugly into his apron.

The guests rushed through the door, giddy to eat lunch after a morning filled with activities. Abe had only a moment to stand back and observe Eugene walking with a new jauntiness.

Wilt strutted into the dining room. He was ready to sit down with the owners at the Kutsher's family table. He had spent the last couple of hours holding court around the hotel and mingling with guests. Last season, he had been a star for the Harlem Globetrotters.

"Bring him matzo ball soup," Abe told a waitress.

"To be in the mountains on a day like today, watching my horse, Rival Time, race at my favorite track . . ." Wilt trailed off, shoveling matzo ball soup into his mouth.

"Get him more," Abe called out to the closest busboy.

Wilt shook it off.

Helen spoke, "he wants to make a quick exit soon. He'll eat everything on the dinner menu later."

Abe smiled, masking his discomfort. He walked away, anxious about whether Hershel was going to cause trouble with the fixed race. The lunch qualified as good, and his staff muscled right through cleanup. Even Eugene participated in cleanup today. He shouted, "goodbye," so lively that everyone had turned his way.

He saw the Brother Team still at their stations after the rest of the staff had already departed. "I was just messin' around when I fired you," he told them.

Brother Number One stepped forward and shook his hand first. Abe was about to turn toward Brother Number Two to shake his hand when Leon walked through the doorway. He swung a bag from the jewelry store in his hands.

"Pour him a cup of coffee," Abe directed Brother Number Two.

"I thought I'd come to see you in action. You'll never believe what I finally found!"

Abe swallowed hard, pretty sure that he knew what Leon was about to reveal. Leon reached into the bag. Sure enough, he held up the only other heart-shaped opal necklace. His grin was proud.

"Well, isn't that something!" Abe feigned shock. He pulled out a chair for his pal as Brother Number Two returned with a cup of coffee resting on a saucer.

Leon dangled the necklace in front of his face. "The entire way over here, I was exasperated with Eva's behavior. Even feeling that way, I couldn't resist peeking into the jewelry store, and thank goodness I did."

Abe touched his thumb to the opal-shaped heart

and pretended it was the first time he had seen the necklace.

"Eva is siding with Hershel. They both think Prince should take first place. Your job is at stake, Abe. My wife should be siding with us, not with her ex." Leon tucked the necklace back into its packaging.

Abe wiped a smudge from his glasses.

"I'm going to splash cold water on my face." Leon took a gulp of coffee and headed toward the washroom. Thirty seconds later, hearing a commotion near the doorway, Abe wondered how Leon could have returned so quickly.

Hershel raced over to him. "We need to get in touch with Sy. It's not easy to admit that I need his help again."

Abe gritted his teeth, gesturing to Hershel and telling the Brother Team, "Get him out of here." A fight between his best pals while his job was brand new was not something he wanted to happen on his watch.

The brothers picked up on the seriousness of the request. Each of them had a hand on an opposite elbow. Hershel jerked his body around and broke free.

"Go, get out of here," Abe yelled at the Brother Team. He understood their hesitation, but he needed them to start running at full speed. Luckily, they did, and Hershel chased them. He crossed his fingers that the two stellar busboys would end up unscathed.

When Leon returned, Abe's heart was thumping. He was afraid Hershel would storm back in at any second, and Abe did not want to have to tell Leon that Hershel intended to give Eva the same necklace he had just purchased. "Why don't you and Eva plan a trip somewhere?" He wanted to suggest something that might be helpful to Leon.

"I'm the maître d' of a busy hotel and it's the busiest season. When will I be able to get away?"

Abe had no rebuttal because he had his own dining room to run and could not offer any assistance. He kept flitting his eyes to the doorway.

Leon wrapped the handle of the jewelry store bag around his wrist. "I'm off to the track to meet Eva."

Brother Number One ran back into the dining room. Brother Number Two kept watch at the door.

Abe liked their dedication. "I'll make you both waiters on Friday. You've earned it."

They thanked him profusely. "Once we make enough tips, we're getting you a bottle of Chivas," Brother Number One called over his shoulder.

Abe shifted his weight from one foot to the other. The Classic was in one hour.

Chapter 55

DOTTY

Dotty grew apprehensive, standing at odds with her friend. She heard a vehicle in the distance and spotted a convertible speed up, then slow down and swerve to avoid them. She held her breath as the blue T-Bird came to a halt.

"Car trouble?"

Eva walked right over to the passenger door and opened it. "We need a ride to the track immediately."

"I'm on my way to the track myself. I took a wrong turn somewhere."

Recognition settled into Dotty's bones. "Ida."

"Norman told me your horse is taking the top prize in the Monticello Classic. I couldn't miss it."

Dotty had no choice but to cram herself in next to Eva, who had always had an affinity for convertibles and was now busy running her hands along the leather seats.

Ida accelerated, slowed down, then sped up again. Clenching and unclenching her hands in her lap, Dotty prayed they would arrive in one piece. Ever since the Route 17 Quickway was completed in 1957, making New York City only 90 miles from the mountains, Ida had come up on a whim whenever the idea popped into her head.

"I don't want to be late," Eva cried.

Ida increased the speed and turned the wheel to the right. Her brimmed straw hat was in danger of blowing off during the quick turn.

"We'll be there in plenty of time. Obey the speed

limit." Dotty glared at Ida. At this point, her only concern was their safety. She vowed to never allow the children in the car with their paternal grandmother behind the wheel.

Eva became the navigator, directing Ida back to the main roads.

"Shtick drek," Ida cursed at the traffic.

It was times like this that made Dotty miss the off-season and the empty roads.

"Some of us want to see our own horse win," Eva jabbed her elbow into Dotty's side.

"That's the beauty of a fixed race—Prince is already the winner. I thought you were the best gambler in the group," Ida cackled.

"This has nothing to do with my gambling record. Wilt Chamberlain's horse winning instead of Prince is all about favoritism," said Eva.

"My son's horse is supposed to win."

"That's right. I'm glad someone other than Hershel finally agrees with me. My husband, Dotty, and Abe are rooting against Prince," Eva grimaced.

"If Abe's boss thinks otherwise, who is my son to go against his superior?"

Dotty was left speechless that Ida had switched her tune and said something in allegiance to Abe.

"Oh, what do you know? You abandoned your kids," Eva spat.

Dotty stiffened.

"My kids were never abandoned. I left them with their father. I was exhausted and felt I deserved a better life, so I took the opportunity. The kids turned out just fine."

No thanks to you, Dotty wanted to add, but for the first time, there was tenderness in Ida's voice. She realized, in her mother-in-law's mind, she had not discarded the children. She had gone away and returned, and that was it.

The radio host raised his voice, "Folks, the news is flying in today. Jack Drucker died in his prison cell on Friday night. The cause of death is listed as a heart attack."

Both of Dotty's hands flew over her mouth. The mystery of why Sy had called and left the cryptic message was solved.

"Ay, ay, ay," Ida yelled, slamming her foot on the brake and stopping right in front of the track.

The pristine racetrack was built for harness racing. Colorful flowers were planted everywhere. Prominent businessmen in the area, including several resort owners, had directorship titles because they had helped with the funding. Arthur Winarick was one of them.

Eva catapulted from the T-Bird. Dotty walked at a slower and steadier pace, processing the news she had heard and preparing herself for the events ahead.

Swinging her handbag over her shoulder, Ida asked, "Who do I need to speak to about the race being fixed?"

Dotty moaned. "Stay by my side." As she searched for Abe in the crowd, catching sight of Leon holding a package tied with a red bow in his hands, she was distracted from keeping tabs on Ida for only a second or two. Locking eyes with Abe, he signaled toward the barn. She was mortified to see her mother-in-law on the move, intent on bribing a driver. Milton Kutsher was taking quick and purposeful strides behind her.

CHAPTER 56

ABE

The energy sizzled. Abe needed to get Ma out of there. Cutting across the grass toward the barn, he saw that Arthur Winarick and Irving Cohen had arrived in time to watch the race. He wished for a hole to crawl into and nearly tripped flat on his face as Hershel ran at him.

"Drucker's dead!"

Abe's heart skipped a beat, but he had to keep going after Ma. "Get us seats!" he yelled to Dotty.

Halfway to the barn, he heard applause behind him. Without slowing down, he glanced over his shoulder to see Wilt Chamberlain waving at the crowd.

Abe was embarrassed to find Ma with a fistful of cash. She was hollering to drivers at the barn's entryway.

"Nobody is allowed access to the horses unless properly supervised," said a man with crossed arms in denim overalls.

"This rule is in effect to protect the horsemen and the horses." Milton Kutsher had one foot inside the barn, glaring.

Ma looked the owner of Kutsher's square in the eye. "I'm on your side. I'm for Rival Time."

Milton stood with a rigid posture and narrowed eyes.

"Even if Prince is the better horse."

Boy, did Abe want to wring her neck over the snide comment. Milton Kutsher left with no more than a nod in his direction. Unable to decipher the meaning behind it, he led his mother toward the bleachers.

"Hello, kid," said a voice from the shadows.

He recognized it instantly. "Stay put," Abe told Ma as he sped over to shake Sy's hand. "Where've you been?"

"I took a slow drive to the Catskills. Visited a gal I knew in grade school along the way. Sometimes I take Hershel's lead and disappear for a couple of nights." He winked. When the mayhem of 1944 took place, Hershel met a waitress twice his age and shacked up with her.

Sy cut right to the chase. "Did you hear Drucker is in his grave?"

Abe nodded his head "yes" as Hershel inched to his side.

"I'm about to ask Rebekah to be my wife. I want to walk into my marriage with a clean slate." He looked at Sy. "It's time I confess."

Sy put a hand on Hershel's shoulder.

"Here's what we've kept secret, Abey. It was the bullet that I shot that killed D.R. Sy didn't murder anybody. It was me."

Abe let what he had just heard sink in. He and Dotty had never discussed the details of that night with anyone. They had both presumed Sy had killed D.R. in self-defense. Here, Hershel was telling him differently. Abe could not quite grasp it all yet. He readjusted his glasses.

"D.R. had a vicious side, so nobody is crying too many tears over his demise," Sy said. "I made Hershel swear that he wouldn't reveal the truth. No matter how much street credibility he thinks it would give him, it could also make him, along with every one of you, a target. We don't need any extra attention on the ordeal.

Only the three of us know the truth, and it should stay that way to keep everyone safe."

Hershel lifted his head. "I can accept that I'll always have blood on my hands because I stopped D.R. from hurting you, Abey."

Now, it makes sense. He was recalling the comment that Hershel had made about being just as good at taking care of business as Sy.

"You don't have to worry about the mysterious skeleton ever again." Sy kneaded his meaty fingers together. "All of the evidence has been destroyed."

If put under oath right then, Abe would say the bones had a likely chance of being D.R.'s. "Where's the fortune?"

"I bet you're thinking who just walks away from that kind of money, kid? After dropping you off at the Concord, I went back up to Rochester to look for it. Unbeknownst to me, D.R.'s sister, Hannah, was up there trying to clean up the mess. She had their mother, who looked prehistoric, drugged on sleeping pills. It was a sight, and I knew they were innocents who needed my help. We decided Hannah would donate the fortune to several worthwhile charities—some good would come out of it at least."

Hershel's jaw hit the ground. "That's where it ended up?!"

Abe would get more of the specific details later; for now, it was enough that the saga was finally over.

"It's almost race time!" shouted a shrill voice. People charged to their seats.

Hershel switched back into racehorse owner mode. "Come on, Prince," he cheered, pumping his fist in the air.

Sy pulled a piece of paper out of his pocket. "It's the top suspects the feds pinpointed as possibly knowing the location of the money. You and Dotty are on it." He tore it apart, and the pieces blew in the wind.

Chapter 57

Abe was leading Ida by the arm to the seats she had saved for them inside the grandstand. It was no easy task with the number of people in attendance.

"Drucker's dead," Abe whispered in her ear.

Due to the noise from the crowd, she asked him to repeat what he had said and then placed her hand over her heart and told him, "I heard the announcement on the radio."

He kept whispering, "The skeleton business was put to bed for good."

Every fiber of her body relaxed. He was saying something about a reliable source, but the packed-to-capacity crowd and commotion everywhere made her unable to hear. She read his lips. "I have a lot to tell you later."

She mouthed back, "and I have a lot to tell you, too."

Ida whacked a fella with her handbag for stepping into her line of vision. Dotty buried her head in her hands, praying Milton was too busy watching the horses to notice.

Laying eyes on their sleek, brown-coated horse, she was confident they had all made the right decisions.

"The race is about to begin. Can you behave yourself a little longer, Ma?" Abe asked.

Dotty stood on her toes as all nine horses trotted out of the starting gate. Her eyes were locked on Prince. She fretted about him having such strong competition.

The race caller's voice boomed from the overhead speaker. He listed the order of the horses before spitting out the progress almost faster than she could keep up.

"Rival Time has the lead by a length. On the outside is Prince in second. Nevele Pride is well placed along the rail in third. From the outside comes Glen Wild in fourth. Ocean Parkway on the far outside is fifth. Latin Dancer comes from the rail in sixth. Summer Season, Gussy Boy, and Romeo are at the back of the pack."

The horses were in the half mile as she looked from Rival Time to Prince. The race caller was shouting at his loudest, "Down the stretch they come!"

"Come on, Prince!" Eva was wildly clapping her hands together.

Leon stood by her side, blowing air out of his cheeks.

"Rival Time, you're almost there," cheered Wilt Chamberlain over the crowd.

Dotty held her breath.

"Prince takes the lead!" the race caller screamed.

She continued to hold her breath.

"Rival Time is right there!" spat the race caller. "Prince on the rail got away!"

A hush blanketed the crowd. Dotty covered her eyes. It was disturbing to see the driver of Glen Wild ahead by 15 lengths, and then suddenly pulling back hard on the horse's reins.

Leon was squinting at the track. "That poor horse."

Ida leaned in. "Races are choreographed ahead of time. You know we're watching a fixed race."

"Look at those two over there. They aren't even pretending not to know the result." Leon stuck his neck out toward the men who were unable to contain their overconfident grins.

"Come on, Rival Time," Dotty silently prayed, wrestling with all sorts of guilt, hoping this would be the last and only time she would have to cheer against Prince. Stealing a peek at Milton, who had his hands on top of his head, she turned back to the track to catch Prince slowing down because his driver was pulling on the reins. Suddenly, Rival Time, too, was trotting without his previous urgency. She focused on the horse galloping on the outside at a very determined speed. Half the crowd was stunned into silence while the other half was flailing about, yelling at the track.

"Nevele Pride crosses the finish line and wins!" declared the race caller.

Ida started elbowing people. She pointed at the track and growled *fakakta* as Nevele Pride trotted triumphantly.

Dotty saw Milton consoling Wilt, with shock and disappointment etched over both their faces. Arthur Winarick and Irving Cohen were not far from them, both cheering for Nevele Pride in disbelief.

Dotty laced her fingers through Abe's and held onto his hand. "A neutral horse winning is the best outcome."

"I can't disagree, Dot." He scanned the crowd. "Someone won a jackpot."

The way he said it made her think he might know exactly who that someone was. As she opened her mouth to ask him about it, Hershel barreled over, shaking his fists.

Eva stepped forward. "Your surefire bet was wrong." She turned her nose up at him.

Hershel scowled. "Abey, that jeweler of yours had better give me a refund." He lumbered off.

Leon took hold of his wife's arm. "I have a surprise for you."

"We have to win in the next pony races to make up for the money we lost," Ida said before staggering off.

Ida and Abe were halfway to the betting booth when the aroma of cigar smoke wafted by Dotty's nose. In the shadows, leaning against an oak tree, she caught Sy's eye. He winked and patted his wallet. "Thank you," she mouthed to the man who had come to their rescue on multiple occasions, glad that he had fixed the race so Abe would keep his job.

Then she simply sat down and breathed in the invigorating mountain air, waiting for the next race to begin. In the distance, she saw Milton approach Abe, and without being able to determine his demeanor, her stomach squirmed.

Eva ran over. "Dotty, you won't believe what Leon gave me!" She brushed her hair off her shoulders to reveal a stunning opal heart on a gold chain.

Dotty oohed and aahed, finding it remarkable how similar the necklace looked to Eva's original one. Still, she remained tense and jiggled her foot as Eva and Leon strolled off arm in arm.

Prince was trotting back to his barn when Abe snuck up behind her. "I have to get over to Kutsher's for dinner soon."

His smile put her at ease. She was so proud of her maître d' husband and raised a hand to wave across the track at Milton. In the distance, right in front of Rebekah, Hershel was on bended knee. Dotty squeezed Abe's arm. All was right in the mountains.

THE END

Acknowledgments

Originally, this book and my debut, *Catskills Capers: Banquets & Bootleg Bounty,* were one big novel. At that point, I thought of it more as historical fiction than a cozy mystery. Karen Hodges Miller helped me figure out the genre and polish it into what it is today. So, everyone I thanked in my first book applies to *Catskills Capers: Mountain Maitre D'* as well. Here's a list; for a more detailed description, see book 1.

I couldn't have done it without you all:

Mom & Dad, Jean Barrish, Kandace Ayala (my star editor), Cassandra Bell, Meredith Schorr, John Conway, Patti Posner, Erica Shawn Gold, Barry Gold, Richard & Jackie Chiger, Myron Gittell, all four of my grandparents, Maggie, Matt, Cameron, Isaac, June, Nick Mullan, Jaycee DeLorenzo, Lisa Snyder, Camille Di Maio, Lucia Macro, Marilyn Simon Rothstein, Thelma Adams, Eva Hnizdo, Sheila Myers. My *bashert,* Jeremy Levner, and our dog, Gus.

There have been a couple more added since then. The baristas at Forage & Gather. All of the program directors that I've reached out to who have helped me set up talks. Eileen Block, my grandma's friend in Rainberry Bay that arranged my book launch there. Evelin Schuster—my cheerleader.

Another huge thank you to my readers. And thank you to everyone who took the time to review my book in any capacity.

In my first book, I didn't mention all the real-life people that I was thinking about while writing. I was fortunate to have so many of my grandparents' friends in my life during my childhood. Spending the summers in the Catskills with them was very special.

Dotty lived to be 88 years old, and Abe lived to be 93 years old. Serendipitously, we buried Grandpa Abe on Grandma Dotty's 89th birthday. They outlived many of their friends.

Dot & Abe's friends who influenced the story:

Jeanie Cove: Waitress at the Concord and then at the Pines.

Bernie Cove: Maître d' at the Pines. He had a Bronze Star Medal and a role in the movie Sweet Lorraine, filmed at the Heiden Hotel.

Helen Kaiser: Waitress at the Concord and my next-door neighbor while I was growing up.

Chick Kaiser: Irving Cohen's assistant maître d'.

Irma Levin: Hairdresser at the Raleigh Hotel.

Jack Levin: Captain of the dining room at the Concord. A tough, muscular guy.

Irving Cohen: Maître d' at the Concord. My neighbor while I was growing up.

Sarah Cohen: Irving's wife and Cub Scout leader.

Leon Rosenberg: Co-captain of the staff dining room at the Concord. He was a refugee from Poland.

Gerta McCormick: Waitress at the Concord. She was a refugee from Austria.

John McCormick: Captain of the dining room at the Concord.

Ruth McGowan: Head ice skater at the Concord.

Doris Steinberg: Her family owned the Rib Room & Pussy Cat Lounge.

Jimmy Steinberg: Hairdresser, married to Doris.

Cookie (real name David Gerson): Sundry Shop

owner at the Concord. My next-door neighbor while growing up.

Tanny Iannone: Waitress at the Concord.

Sonny Rossi: Tanny's husband and bandleader at the Concord.

Fran Stoloff: She was married to Abe's brother Al. In real life, Al lived to be 29 years old and died from prostate cancer. For the story's sake, I moved his death a decade earlier to World War II in my first book.

Jerry Stoloff: He became Uncle Jerry when Fran married him.

Murray Stock: The oldest friend of my grandpa that I ever met. They knew each other from Brooklyn.

Fannie Silvers: Owner of Silvers Bungalow Colony.

Gwen Silvers: Fannie's daughter. She worked at the jewelry counter at the Concord.

Abe Rosenberg: Insurance agent.

Rebecca Rosenberg: She and her husband owned a country home in Bethel, as well as their Monticello house. My grandparents used to take me there.

ABOUT THE AUTHOR

Lily Barrish Levner comes from a family that cherished books and learning—her mother was a schoolteacher, and her father was the director of the Monticello, New York, Library, so it's no surprise that storytelling has always been a part of her life. Growing up in Kiamesha Lake, New York, Lily spent her childhood sleuthing around the iconic Catskills resorts with friends and soaking up the vibrant atmosphere. Her grandparents worked in the resort industry, a connection that inspires her stories.

As a fourth-generation Jewish American, Lily deeply connects to the Catskill Mountains and the Borscht Belt, where her heritage and childhood memories blend. Her fondest recollections are tied to places such as the Concord, Kutsher's, the Pines, the Raleigh, and Sunny Oaks bungalow colony—sites that have left an indelible mark on her writing.

With a BA in Creative Writing and a Master's in Library and Information Science, Lily has spent the past decade as a copy desk researcher at *Bloomberg Businessweek* while working on her novels and contributing monthly articles to the *Hurleyville Sentinel*. She currently lives in the Catskills with her husband and their dog, Gus, where the magic of the mountains still influences her work.

Stay tuned for the further adventures of Dotty and Abe in the third installment of the *Catskills Capers* series—*Woodstock Waitress Whodunit*.